Royce Keaveney, he/him

Free Like You

A Novel of Unabashed Queerness

Copyright © 2021 by Royce Keaveney

First paperback edition - 2021

Book design by Royce Keaveney

ISBN 9798736108473

Please follow Royce Keaveney @

 @Royce_Keaveney

 @royce_keaveney

For more information, please write to
Royce_keaveney@hotmail.com

Author's Note

I chose to write this novel for reasons which would be predictably typical of most authors. The first and foremost is that the subject matter resonates with me on a personal level, I find the characters to be cathartic avatars, and I enjoy commenting on imbalances and unfairness in the world as I see it.

The second reason, just as typical as the first, is that I wanted to work through a drinking problem.

Actually, "problem" may be a strong word. More fair to say that the prospect of maintaining social distance throughout a global pandemic would have caused me to intensify my already apparent drinking habit and, finding this prospect undesirable, I opted to stay busy.

Whichever of those reasons you find most relatable, for better or for worse, this novel is now complete. I hope that when you read it, you feel that you're with company and that your problems are surmountable.

Above all else, I hope this novel is as kind to your liver as it was to mine.

For Blondie, the bravest person I know.

Chapter 1

Wherein we head
out and the
vibration takes
hold.

(1)

Vibration. The first sensory accompaniment to a night out is joined immediately by music, the dense smell of bodies and nurturing lights.

Deep in that interweave of sensory festivity, stood Jamie. Elbows perched playfully on the bar, they were observing the preparation of a double gin and soda. An older gentleman, the purchaser of this particular libation, stood close to Jamie. Close enough to let his cologne share in his flirtatious efforts. It was sharp, expensive and masculine, and Jamie could not help but lean in closer. They also liked his neat moustache and muscular forearms.

"I absolutely love the look," the gentleman said with the confident flattery of a seasoned prospector.

Jamie smiled a perfect, youthful smile. Raising a hand to their face in false modesty, their new, pink acrylic nails just barely made contact with their meticulously shaped eyebrows. "Oh my God, stop. Thank you."

For Jamie, the choice was modesty or a reserved confidence.

"I actually do think that I look really good tonight," they said, knowing that modesty was for the daytime. Reservation, too, for that matter.

Jamie's new purveyor of drinks flexed his forearms before speaking. Jamie couldn't help but notice and wondered if he was doing it on purpose.

"You're absolutely right, you do. Those jeans are absolutely painted on. How do you manage to get into them?" he asked.

"It takes time, but these jeans have paid for themselves several times over in drinks. Enough liquid lunches to keep me in a twenty-six-inch waist."

Jamie's new, handsome bar friend laughed and moved a large hand to the precariously sensual area of Jamie's hip, just below the bare skin between their skin-tight jeans and crop top T-shirt. "I wasn't even that slim when I was in my twenties."

Being nineteen years old, Jamie couldn't relate but they let it slide without correction. After all, this one was cute, and along with his clumsy wantonness came the prospect of a reprieve from loneliness and the fulfilment of a basic need. Jamie stared into his eyes and at the deep, experienced lines that stretched to his temple. Taking another deep breath of that cologne and feeling the warmth of his palm on their hip, Jamie was more than considering a dalliance risqué. If only he had stopped speaking at that point.

"Plus, I absolutely love femboys."

The acrid and overbearing concoction of this conversation was suddenly as evident to Jamie as the cheap, over-applied cologne hanging in the air. A conversation lifeboat arrived just in time in the guise of a complete and paid for double gin and soda. Proof that there is a God and she has no time for this conversation. Jamie took a sip and then turned their body, effectively displacing the encroaching hand of false promises. "It's really good. I have to go find my friends. Thanks again."

Those muscular forearms tensed in desperation. "No, stay with me for a whi—"

"Have a great night!" interrupted Jamie as they made their easy escape. A quick turn and they could blend easily into the crowd of bodies shuffling and moving from prospect to prospect. Ascending the neon stairs, Jamie arrived onto the second floor of Quake. Nestled between a solicitors' office and a convenience shop, inside its opulent walls and among its three floors, it contained the combined queer majesty of all recorded time. Such was the duty of all queer spaces.

A survey of the crowd was unnecessary as Jamie's friends were exactly where they had left them. Escape was impossible during one of Akib's rants.

"It's like chocolate," said Akib, obviously at the end of a point. Across from them in the booth were Shira, Coach and Ren.

"Chocolate, as in something you can't have?" asked Coach.

"Enough vegan jokes," replied Akib. "No, chocolate as in different types of chocolate. Everyone likes it but variety is what drives it forward."

"Variety in what, honey-boo?" asked Jamie while returning to their place among the booth's inhabitants. The new drink in their hand went unquestioned.

"Oh, you're back. I was just saying that I was

speaking to this guy online last night and eventually we started talking about queer stuff in our areas. Anyway, he tells me that he doesn't really understand why we need so many terms. Like, he doesn't know why we needed stuff like omnisexual or pansexual and gender fluid and intersex and so many others when we could all just plant ourselves under the label of being queer. The sheer scope of the human experience seemed to confuse the poor, handsome moron."

"Oh, well we do stan a handsome moron but that is quite a lot. What did you tell him?"

"I didn't tell him anything. I only rant at people that I care about. That's why I'm here talking to you folks." The group smiled while Shira almost lost her drink from snorting with laughter. "As cruel as it may seem," Akib continued, "it's true. Anyway, I was saying that even if we did have one big, all-encompassing word to use, we should still continue to clarify new ones. Frankly, I can't wait for the next one. A new people about which to learn and a new little subculture to explore."

Jamie loved listening to Akib when they were like this. Five years of friendship, three foreign trips together, six music festivals, seventeen drunken kisses, two fumblings and one far-too sober romantic episode had transpired between them and Jamie never grew tired of their conviction.

"See, that's what I get for talking with boys online. You know, when I came out as trans and started to transition, I was determined to be the best man I could be. Then, after only a brief time, I realised that the bar had been set pretty low. Maybe I have too much time on my hands. Contouring is time-consuming and I don't listen to music while in the act. Gives one time to think." Akib raised a delicate hand to their well-structured face, making sure to look away in profile.

Jamie complied and gasped in admiration. "Yas, my Gawd, look at this. Now, as much as I'm afraid that you'll cut me with those cheek bones, I do see where your handsome moron is coming from. A few years ago, our little group would have been pretty diverse. Now, the most interesting thing about us is that we have two single lesbians."

"We're not pandas in a zoo," insisted Coach. "You don't just put us together and we start to mate."

"Actually, Coach, that's something that they find notoriously difficult with pandas in zoos," said Shira.

"Oh, that's right. Okay, then we are like pandas in a zoo."

Shira smiled a wonderfully crooked smile in agreement. "Coach is right. Plus, we're trying to do away with that whole U-Haul image. No cats either. I actually prefer dogs anyway."

"While I just hate pets altogether."

Akib jumped on that last point, of course. Coach had brought it on herself. Jamie was sipping their well-earned drink through smiling lips. A roaming glance at the room gave way to more promises for the night: the hairy brunette in the corner with boulders for shoulders; the couple dancing with groggy abandon near the smoking area; the Asian hunk across the room sporting a recently shaven Mohawk. Jamie wondered what it would feel like to the touch.

Much like hair, was the answer.

Jamie noticed that Ren had joined them in the room surveillance. This was, after all, what Ren was good at. The almost permanently silent member of the group smiled at jokes and offered advice when asked but what they wanted from nights like this was the connection. Jamie had seen it time and time again. Ren would rise of their own accord, brush the dark hair from in front of their green eyes and walk over to a worthy recipient. Never anyone who was drunk, never anyone who was exposed and never the same person twice. A few whispers in their ear and they were with Ren now.

They had come to the group the same way they came to everyone – without a surname, without origin, without preferences or baggage of any kind. Adrift on a nightly raft of carefree pleasures. *An inspiration for us all,* Jamie thought, *if such a thing even exists.*

Jamie looked at Ren, took in the familiar sight of their minimalist, post-punk aesthetic and smiled a genuine smile. Eyes and all. Ren responded in kind and even raised the platonic stakes with a wink. Jamie's heart fluttered just a tad and that was that.

By now, the spill over from the dance floor had very much engulfed the area around Jamie's table. The rhythmic ruminations of bodies whispered out for growth.

Soon, Jamie thought, *but not yet.*

Looking down, they could see the varied footwear

moving beautifully, in and out of unison with the music. One pair stood out. Perched right in front of Jamie were the unmistakeable, size 11, well-polished, red-laced, 14-eyelet Doc Marten boots belonging to Orion.

"Orion!" exclaimed Jamie while placing their empty glass down and arising from their stool. Orion's welcoming figure was visible even under Quake's shimmering illumination, his round, muscular form fitting well with his 6'3 vertical endowment. The clear whites of his brown eyes contrasted tenderly with his dark skin. Jamie also noted that he had grown a beard since they had last met.

"Hey, you. Long time, no scene" said Orion with characteristic warmth. Jamie flung their comparatively tiny frame into Orion's open arms; he responded by lifting Jamie two feet into the air with ease. Face to face and in the reassuring embrace of a muscular bear hug, Jamie felt delicate and adored. A quick kiss on the lips before Jamie was returned safely to the floor. The vibration returned once again to meet them through their shoes.

"I love being lifted. Makes me feel precious. Orion, it's great to see you. You look absolutely amazing. You've really bulked up." Jamie groped the outside of Orion's sizeable arm and gave a firm squeeze. Orion flexed his bicep in compliance. "Yas! The boots and the muscles. You're serving some Daddy dom realness."

Jamie was drunk but also correct. Over the last year, Orion had embraced a socially acceptable leather aesthetic. Along with his boots, he sported some tight leather jeans, a red trimmed leather wrist wallet and a small black waistcoat over a sleeveless white T-shirt. Hanging around his neck was a plain, thick, metal chain with a silver padlock. Jamie wondered where the key was but decided not to ask. "So, where have you been hiding yourself these days, except the gym and whatever ethical leather emporium you frequent?"

Then it came back to them. This was the first time Jamie had seen Orion in months but was also the first time since Orion's little episode. It had happened in Quake, midday and during a weekly bingo session. Jamie remembered that Orion had been quiet all evening and then, during one of Akib's rants on the negative effects of emojis on modern speech, excused himself for the bathroom. Thirty minutes later, Coach took Jamie aside and told them that Orion was sitting in the closed bathroom stall but was not responding to anyone. Cut to ten minutes later and Peter, the third most handsome bouncer in Quake, was knocking on the bathroom door. Jamie watched as Orion, never saying a word, opened the stall door, gently moved everyone aside and walked out of the building. His jacket and satchel remained as a clue that something terrible had happened. Among the group, Only Ren was silent in their hypothesising.

Orion did speak out eventually. He contacted Jamie a few days later and explained that he had experienced an anxiety attack somewhere during the intermission of banter between two bingo drag queens. Everyone responded with genuine sympathy, but the topic definitely remained a point of discussion for a week at least. Jamie wondered how such a thing could have slipped their mind.

(The answer was gin.)

Still, that was months ago. Perhaps Orion didn't want to dwell.

"I've been in therapy, mainly."

Never mind.

"I don't mean to get serious, I just thought I'd address the obvious but ya, I've been to a therapist a few times over the past months and like you said, I've been exercising and finding new interests," he said, holding the large lock hanging from his neck. "So ya it's all really been helping, and I've been feeling a lot better. Like myself but older."

"Dear God, that last part sounds awful."

"Oh, it is but no worse than anyone else. So, how have you been doing, you little ageless sprite?"

"Good," answered Jamie. "Much the same and fabulous as ever. I had my hair done a month ago but need to go again soon. I got my second tattoo on my ribs and I'm saving up for a third, and I'm still looking for a salon in the city that's looking for an apprentice."

"You're still looking? I thought you would have found something by now."

"I know, it's terrible," said Jamie suddenly wishing there was a drink in their hand. "I've been looking for a while but it's the modern day so there's a makeup queen on every corner these days. Makes you want to give up and set up an OnlyFans."

Orion laughed at Jamie's half joke. "Trust me, those

never last for long. Have you ever thought of—"

"Going back to do another course?" interrupted Jamie. "Ya I have but I dunno. I kind of like how things are going for me at the moment." Jamie suddenly wished they had a drink in both hands. Best to change the subject. "So, is this your first time back since the bathroom drama?"

"I'm sure we've both had worse times in that bathroom but yes, this is the first time back. I missed everyone and the vibration. Things look fairly familiar."

"Do you want to go take a look?" Jamie took hold of Orion's hand and moved to a nearby wall so as to better rest their poor queer backs. From here, they could see the entire second floor. Orion was right, things did look familiar. Newbies danced meekly on the dance floor, too scared to seek the attention they had been told they deserve. A figure known colloquially as 'Shirtless guy' roamed bare-chested across the room, as free as an animal and brave as a Gurkha. A group of well-offs stood in their smart-casual attire, all malice and pretention left outside these sacred walls. Sidney, the most handsome bouncer, lurked on the outskirts looking for breaches of Quake's already very lax rules. Queens fended off chasers with jagged swords of wit and bodily autonomy. Bears conversed with twinks. Fems laughed with mascs. Otters, wolves, polar bears, closet cases, daddies, leather lovers, rubber boys, pups, manatees, chem-queers, scene kids, alt-queens. Colour, shape, age. Never before had one group encompassed so many and Jamie loved it. They felt strong, as if they may uncharacteristically bang their chest and let out a primal scream. If there was any grace to be drawn from diversity, this was it.

Then, everything went dark. The vibration remained but it was dark all the same. Two overly familiar hands had been placed over Jamie's eyes.

"Guess who?" asked the hand's owner.

"RuPaul?" answered Jamie.

"No, it's me."

The figure was instantly recognisable.

"Oh, Barry, it's you. I should have guessed." Jamie was sure that Orion could detect the slight forced enthusiasm in their voice.

"Well, aren't you sweet," said Barry and the two shared a hug. Jamie noted that Barry smelled of unassuming soap and had slightly more grey hairs than their last encounter. "RuPaul is the drag queen, right?"

"That's right, Barry. Have you met Orion before?"

"Not in person," said Barry, shaking Orion's hand, "but maybe online."

Unlikely, Jamie thought as Barry had no online presence save for one blank profile on a gay hook-up app.

"So," said Barry, returning his attention to Jamie, "what have you been up to lately?"

Jamie was used to this. To Barry, Jamie was a strange, exciting young thing full of queer majesty. Barry insisted on this ritual every time their paths crossed. It was slightly flattering and slightly objectifying. Either way, Jamie had long since embraced the act of embellishment for creative effect.

"What have I been up to? Recently, my friend Akib and I were volunteering at a queer youth program in their gender acceptance classes. Then, our friend Shira brought us to her lesbian poetry showcase. My God, so many metaphors involving flowers."

Jamie could see that they were losing their audience.

"Then, a few days after, Akib and I were discussing setting up a joint OnlyFans when we accidently had too much to drink at two in the afternoon so, naturally, we spent the day trying on heels and doing our makeup. Eventually, we went out like that and ran into some guys from the local gay rugby club and they invited us to a house party. It was fun but we left when things got a little steamy."

Saved it with the ending, Jamie could tell from Barry's face. "But anyway, how are you?"

Jamie had repeated this ritual with Barry several times now and not once had Barry responded with any form of content. This time was no exception.

"Oh, I'm good. Not been up to much so not much to tell."

That was that. The ritual complete and the virgin sacrificed. Jamie smiled and allowed the silence to linger just long enough to be noticeable. Barry blinked first which was ironic as Jamie's fake eyelashes were causing them a minor eye irritation. Another awkward hug and handshake before Barry wished them a good night and descended a nearby staircase.

"He's something of an eager fellow," quipped Orion

with a gentle cockiness that Jamie had missed.

"Oh, don't start. We met a few months ago and he just seems to appear every night that I'm here and is always very curious about what I'm doing and who I think is hot. I think he draws life from my age-to-queerness ratio like some precarious poltergeist."

"So, how much of that story was true?"

"All of it except the ending."

"There was no steam?"

"Oh, there was steam a plenty, but it was a non-descript crowd at the house party and we were there without an invitation. You know that we'd never hang with the gay rugby crew. Exclusionary meatheads."

"How do you get into places without an invite?"

Jamie stepped closer to Orion, grabbed his bicep, and produced their best voice of excitable absent-mindedness. "Oh my god, Orion, you have the biggest biceps." A slight giggle and Jamie returned to their regular, only slightly absent-minded ways. "Just like that."

"Point taken."

Jamie and Orion went on like that for some time, about the length of three Gloria Gaynor remixes. They asked about mutual friends, congratulated recent victories, and dismissed each other's losses. Jamie could not help but look at Orion as he spoke with the kind of look one would attribute to a tourist in the Louvre. The surrounding, multi-coloured lights were moving over Orion, highlighting his masculine features. The stubble on his chin and the almost perfect lines around his eyes.

Inebriated or not, Jamie was transfixed. Nothing like some mutual physical appreciation between friends.

After a goodbye kiss on the cheek, Jamie was given the last word. "Don't be a stranger," was all they could muster. Orion returned the favour with a wave and a smile of those perfect teeth before turning to walk away, the tail end of which Jamie took an unashamed moment to appreciate.

Standing alone, Jamie felt suddenly self-conscious. Their interaction with Orion was more than welcome but it did serve to highlight his previous absence. When thinking of the time Orion was forced to keep his distance from them, Jamie was filled with a very human mix of ninety-five percent compassion and five percent annoyance. Those numbers left them feeling cold. Something was needed to warm the blood.

Jamie's legs, whether suitable for the journey or not, carried them past the treacherously familiar landscapes that lay ahead. Across the enticing dance floor, down the dizzying staircase, past the gyrating natives and over and under any sense of prevailing moral consensus. Finally, Jamie reached their crowded oasis, just barely managing to squeeze to the front. The annoyingly handsome bartender asked Jamie for their order, giving no indication of anything other than busy professionalism. This, after all, was the handsome bartender way.

Jamie returned the favour.

"Double vodka and Red Bull, please."

Less than twenty cold and silent seconds later, the drink was in Jamie's hands. Gently tapping on the glass with their painstakingly applied nails, Jamie watched the bubbles rise and burst out like circuit twinks on a long weekend. *The La-Fit 45 again? I really must switch to champagne,* Jamie thought before downing a sizeable gulp. A *drink never tastes as good if you buy it yourself.* A remnant of Jamie's face remained on the glass. Stains sponsored by L'Oréal.

"You must be trying to get there pretty fast."

The statement came from beside them. They stood with their elbows on the bar, surveying the customers lined up on the opposite side.

"Where am I trying to go?"

They turned themselves away from the bar and directly toward Jamie. "Wherever it is that vodka Red Bull brings you, friend."

"Let's just say it's my happy place."

"Ya, I remember being nineteen as well. I'm Caoimhe she/her. I love your makeup, by the way. Who did it for you?"

Jamie liked this one.

"I'm Jamie they/them and this," said Jamie while striking a statuesque pose, "is a home creation. Face by Jamie and one hundred percent all unnatural. Just as God intended."

Caoimhe laughed a short, loud yelp. Jamie liked it. In fact, Jamie liked a lot about Caoimhe. She was older by at least five years and easily stood six inches over Jamie. Her deep, black hair reached her shoulders and framed her beautifully pale face. She wore a sleeveless shirt with some band Jamie didn't recognise. Jamie counted the number of visible piercings they could see. Six. A good number compared to Jamie's four. Then there were her hands.

"Oh my God, girl, stop!" Jamie reached forward and took hold of Caoimhe's hand. "Are these Tulip Destiny nails in obsidian?"

"Yes!" said Caoimhe through a delighted laugh. "It's nice to finally be appreciated for my amazing taste as well as my good looks."

Jamie's turn to laugh a short yelp. "It must be nice when that happens to you, you absolute diva of humility. Now, tell me tell me, tell Jamie where you found these nails? I've been scouting everywhere."

Caoimhe pouted her lips and retrieved her hand from Jamie's admiring examination.

"Sorry, beautiful. As tempted as I am to extort a drink out of you for the information, I like you, so I'll be honest and tell you that my friend picked them up overseas. Complete fluke. Couldn't get more if I wanted to. These," Caoimhe mimicked Jamie's earlier pose, "are all we have."

"Oh, boo. That means I'll have to move on with nothing but hope and these ratchet claws I call hands …" Jamie paused to take another sizeable gulp in their journey.

"So, Caoimhe with the nice nails, what brings you to our little club tonight?"

"Girl's night," was all Caoimhe would give away as if she didn't know that was an extremely annoying answer. "Now, you're probably wondering where all my girls are. I'm sad to say they couldn't even make it past midnight. That's why I like coming here. This club has stamina. A little perseverance can go a long way."

"Must be in our DNA. Listen, girl, we've been hogging this bar space for over two minutes now. That's an eternity in alcohol adjacent real estate. I'm going to head up to my friends. You should come with me."

Jamie wasn't sure why they'd just blurted a random invitation. Their friend group was by no means exclusionary, but they also knew all too well how an unwelcome guest could put a downer on a night. Still, they were confident. Well not confident, drunk, but at three in the morning, who could tell the difference? Plus, if things went well, Jamie could ply her with booze and rip those nails right off.

Just a thought, of course.

"Go upstairs?" she asked. "Are you sure you wouldn't rather stay down here and check out some man folk?"

"There's a time for man folk and there's a time for making sure your friends know you're not sprawled out on the bathroom floor. Now come on. I'm only tiny and these drinks are strong. I may need some help up these stairs."

Jamie held out a hand which Caoimhe accepted.

What followed was an hour or so of sensory input. More lights, more noise, more vibration. Flashing, laughing, bubbles. So many bubbles. This was the period where people made peace with their night. Was it good, was it disappointing and most importantly, was it over? The choices that every single person made that night in that crowded club were gathering to greet them. A most unwelcome time of reflection. Jamie and their friends had long since developed an immunity. Fuelled by a youthful desire to hold onto the night, they pushed forward with no clock to dictate and no worries to distract.

Caoimhe fit right in, of course. She debated with Akib and joined Coach and Shira in speculating about Ren's backstory. After a while, Jamie noticed something. Something brand new. Caoimhe was looking at them. Not a glance or even a stare but definitely a look. They had seen it before, of course, but never from a woman. Peeking up from below her dark eyelashes, Jamie could not help but meet her dark green eyes. They seemed to move and blink and become surrounded by smile wrinkles in unison with the vibration of the building. The entire night was contained there in those eyes. When she laughed, Jamie laughed. When she asked a question, Jamie answered. Finally, when she suggested that they go dance, Jamie was first to the dance floor.

Slow down, Jamie thought. *Calm down, you messy queen.*

The dance floor was crowded so they danced close together. Jamie and Caoimhe. The other people on the floor weren't really people at all anymore. They weren't really there. Not like Caoimhe was. She was a constant interruption.

Calm down. I wonder, should I get another drink?

Ya, but Caoimhe's wrists, though.

That guy in the muscle shirt is definitely looking at me from across the room. I wonder should—?

Ya, but Caoimhe's hair, though.

This is definitely weird. Maybe more booze isn't the answer.

Ya, but Caoimhe's dance moves, though. Her voice, her nose, her hips and her neck. This must be how the other half lives.

The pretence of looking had long since ended. Jamie and Caoimhe were staring into each other's eyes. Both sets of hands were touching bare skin.

Jamie felt exposed. Caoimhe bent her head down to meet Jamie's ear and whispered something ambitious. Finding it agreeable, Jamie finally fully let go.

No more interruptions.

It was now Caoimhe's turn to hold out a hand. Jamie accepted, pausing to admire those precious and rare nails one last time. The two almost fell into hysterics as they eschewed the cloakroom and instead moved straight for a nearby taxi rank. Soon, Jamie found themselves in a dark and messy apartment, God knows how far from the club. It didn't matter though, Caoimhe was there and after two hours of matching each other drink for drink, neither was in any state to have too many concerns. After some giggling and gossiping, they found themselves lying next to each other. Jamie looked into her eyes with innocent intent for the last time. She smiled and that was it.

What started with vibrations had ended here. Less

than seven hours ago, Jamie had been perched in front of their mirror, applying makeup, and deciding who they wanted to be for the night. An all-too-familiar setting. This was not familiar. This was foreign and exciting and new.

So very new.

She took them in her hands and, in spite of whatever night they had planned previously, Jamie became a happy and willing pilgrim in this new land. All pretence they had amassed for the night was destroyed. Any protection they had prepared, broken.

An omen of things to come, for sure.

Free Like You

<u>Chapter 2</u>

Wherein people are definitely talking about us.

(2)

Orion was always reassured by Dr Fallon's office. The light blue walls were adorned with pictures of loved ones and was far from the cold, analytical setting he had expected when he arrived for his first therapy session. No therapist's couch, no imposing desk and no clock. Just a simple and plain blue room populated with several comfy armchairs, a station for hot drinks and one dedicated therapist.

Several weeks had passed now since that first session. Orion was timid for sure, but he was no fool. After his quite severe panic attack in Quake and the days of depression that followed, he decided to seek help. A simple referral and he had found himself sitting in one of Dr Fallon's comfy armchairs. In private moments, Orion would look back to that first session. So deep was his confusion that he could refer to his attack only as 'the incident'. Dr Fallon quickly disavowed Orion of this denial and soon, the normalising effect of regular sessions with a compassionate professional had yielded positive results.

Today's session would hopefully continue that trend.

"So, Orion," said Dr Fallon, leaning back into her regular chair and cradling a large mug with both hands.

"Since we last spoke, you went out to attempt to meet with old friends and return to your regular social spaces. How was that?"

Orion thought back to his recent visit to Quake. After catching up with Jamie, he had wandered the neon-bathed floors for a while. Eventually, he found himself perched on the top floor balcony from which one could look down on fellow patrons. To the untrained eye, it appeared to be a writhing, dancing ocean of bodies. Orion, however, could recognise the cliques. The mechanics of an after-hours queer space were no mystery to him. What annoyed him the most was the blissful indifference of it all. From here he could see who was being avoided, who was being excluded, who was being taken advantage of and none of it seemed to bother any of them. No one was dejected by being subtly excluded from the popular group or insulted that their nightly companion was searching for a more seductive prospect. As far as Orion could see, everyone in that vibrating pit had the supernatural ability to have a good time despite circumstances to the contrary.

This phenomenon had done more than frustrate Orion; it had exhausted him. Catching up with Jamie had been nice and he was proud of himself for the step this visit represented in his therapy, but Orion could summon no more energy with which to scrutinise these people. He had taken one last masochistic glance at the crowd and then headed for the exit. On the way home, he couldn't help but self-criticise for not staying longer.

"I'd say it was a mixed bag," answered Orion. Dr

Fallon's kind nod and silence were an invitation to continue.

"Okay, so I'm out and meeting people and treating the whole thing in what I assume you would call a very cautious way and it was all going well. As the night went on though, I couldn't help feeling trapped and a bit nervous."

"Trapped?" asked Dr Fallon. "That's quite interesting. You've never described your emotional state like that before. Can you expand on that?"

"Not trapped as in claustrophobia or a fire hazard or anything so morbid. Trapped as in a …" Orion paused to stare down for a moment into the dark and reflective contents of his mug. "When I first started going out in queer spaces, I never thought I was the most fun. I mean, I like to have fun, of course, but I can feel awkward and there are certain things that come naturally to people that terrify me. Also, when I am relatively happy in social spaces, I can't help but look around and think that a different group or crowd are having more fun and are intentionally excluding me somehow and I always thought that everybody does this. Sometimes it can annoy me when I see people unaware of when they are supposed to be having a bad time. Anyway, when I was out last week, I was looking at the crowd. I was alone, thank God, so I was able to just think for a while and as I was thinking, I noticed the people that seemed to be having the most fun very naturally fit into a type."

"What type is that?"

"Young, thin, very expressive and excitable with

lots of gender fluidity."

"So does their gender fluidity make you feel uncomfortable or threaten you in some way?"

"God, no. No, this isn't that conversation."

Dr Fallon furrowed her brow and placed her still half-full mug on the small table next to her. "What conversation is this then? You're commenting on these physical aspects in a way that would make you seem envious, but we've discussed body issues in the past and you said that you're very happy with your physical appearance."

"Yes, we did and yes, I definitely am. It's not like that. It's just that there's so much diversity in scene now and with that comes so much expression and identities and I've always been me. A run-of-the-mill gay with pretty masculine features and yes, before you say anything, I know that comes with a lot of privilege.."

"Ya, I wasn't going to say that."

"Oh, sorry. Well, it is true and I recognise that. I probably won't face a lot of prejudice and even just being physically strong has its advantages. I just feel that I've always been typecast as that guy. Masculine, strong and boring. I never got to cross-dress or paint my nails or wear something revealing at a Pride parade."

"And this is because you feel you won't be accepted because of the role into which you've been assigned by your culture?"

"No, that's the worst part. I haven't been assigned anything. There's no external force. When I was out, I saw guys much more masculine than me doing the kind of stuff I never got to do. I know no one would judge me but when I think about expressing my queer side in a way that I might enjoy but which I'm not really used to, I become anxious. I think that as I've gotten through my twenties, I've had so many opportunities to do something – get on a stage or show off in some way – something to show that I'm here and I'm a beautiful, queer person. But whenever I do, whenever I imagine myself among the young, excitable crowds, I get anxious, I feel exhausted and then I have a panic attack in a nightclub bathroom, and all this happens because I've built up this image of myself in my head and I can't get away from it because I think I'm just a fundamentally scared person."

Orion finally looked up from his now cold drink to meet Dr Fallon's eyes. "And I think it makes sense for someone who's scared all the time to feel trapped."

Prior to his first session, this nature of self-reflective confession would have been impossible for Orion. The relationship would have been too reminiscent of a religious ceremony where sins of thought and failure of character were laid bare for penance. Orion despised useless things and that form of admission provided no growth or change.

For him, these sessions with Dr Fallon had proved far from useless. A confession without judgement or penance was a rare and precious thing. Each time Orion indulged and divulged his fears and fantasies, he could feel himself rise further from the warm and dark void in his ego. Even now, at the conclusion of his most recent disclosure, he felt no shame and erected no barricade.

"Orion, first of all, I want to tell you something that I'm sure you already know. Those feelings are perfectly natural and very common in some form or another."

"Actually, I didn't know that second part."

"Oh, sure. I mean, everybody forms images of themselves in their head. The image of someone they are or someone they want to be and it's perfectly natural to let that image help guide our ambitions and the limitations we set for ourselves. The problem is that some people have an image of themselves that they don't particularly like and this is where one can enter a dangerous territory because if we believe that the image we have of ourselves doesn't deserve to be happy, well that can have dangerous effects on our health."

"Are you saying that I just don't like myself?"

Dr Fallon took a pause and an inward breath before answering. "No, I don't think it's as simple as that. I've known you for a while now and from what you've always told me, you seem to have well-developed self-confidence. No, I just think that you seem to have consulted with that image of yourself and you both seem to have decided that you're allowed to be happy but you're not allowed to go through any emotional development."

Orion placed his own mug on the side table by the chair, leaned back into his armchair and crossed his legs without saying a word.

"Not satisfied?" asked Dr Fallon.

"No, just seems a bit light on details."

"Agreed, and I was definitely planning to leave it at that. Having been a professional therapist for twenty-three years, I am notoriously vague in my summations."

"We're employing sarcasm in our sessions now?"

"The first time's free. Any more will cost extra. However, I do find it interesting that you claim to have reached this emotional state all by yourself with no external influence. We've spoken a bit about this in the past but tell me how you feel you being a person of colour fits into this image of yourself."

The question certainly took Orion by surprise. Dr Fallon was correct in that they had discussed his racial identity and what it meant to him in past sessions but only when detailing the pride it awarded him. He was, as far as he was aware, one of only a few people with both Nigerian and Brazilian heritage on the local scene. "What do you mean by that?" he asked in his least accusatory tone.

"To me, it sounds like we're discussing how you feel stuck in your image of yourself, almost typecast to act a certain way. I feel it would be naïve to ignore the external influence of a queer scene often dominated by a white majority."

"You make it sound like some troubled colony."

"Be that as it may, I think it's something that you've probably thought of in the past and probably more so during the last few months."

She was correct again, of course. Orion held no double thought on the matter. No shame and no self-hatred.

He knew that he was beautiful.

He knew his skin was beautiful. His hair was beautiful. His eyes and nose and mouth were beautiful. His history and culture were beautiful. Every poem and every song in its own unique way. He neither wanted nor needed any confirmation to know all this was true. This beauty granted Orion so much pride and so, conversely, his recent thoughts had caused him much distress.

"I don't think it's racism. Let me just start with that. Everyone on the scene has always treated me with respect. However, I can't deny that I am often treated a certain way and it can be distressing."

"What way is that?"

"Okay, well, say if I'm talking to a guy and maybe things are going well. After a while it becomes obvious that he thinks – just because of my race – that I'm supposed to be very masculine and aggressive and other things that he wants."

"And why, in particular, do you feel that bothers you?"

"Two reasons, I suppose. The first is that I'm insulted this other guy only wants to get with some masculine caveman. I mean, I know preferences exist but most of the kind of guys he's after are about as boring as rugby. Secondly, it limits me. I'm not a person with potential anymore. I've been reduced to a large, masc, black guy. They don't need to say it, you know. I can see it in their eyes and hear it in the way they talk to me."

Unbeknownst to Orion, he had moved from his leaned back position to sitting forward, emphasising every perceived slight with his hands. "And do you know how many guys have actually told me that they liked me because they love seeing black guys in porn?"

"That can't possibly be true?"

"It is!" insisted Orion. "Guys have said that to me and it creeps me out every time, and do you know who black guys never get to be in porn?"

"Who?"

"The husband!"

Dr Fallon looked for a moment as if she might respond to that but instead made a small scribble on her notepad. Orion had grown to despise this.

"What note could you possibly be making from that?"

Continuing to look down at her pad, she answered, "Nothing. This is just the first time that you've mentioned marriage in any way."

"I can't believe that is what you got from what I just said. This isn't about marriage and it certainly isn't about porn. It's about me not having the chance to explore any other persona or even a different mood. I have to constantly be chasing and driving the situation. I never get to be pursued or charmed. To be, you know … delicate just for once. Just for a little while." Sinking back into the chair, Orion looked at a section of blue wall to his side where he always though a window should be. "Just once I'd like to be passive or submissive both in and out of the bedroom. There's nothing wrong with it you know; it takes great trust. It's probably a great relief just for a short period but to be honest, the whole idea terrifies me. I'm expected to dominate and the whole thing is repetitive and exhausting."

A small group of distant birds flew across the outside of Orion's imaginary window.

He could feel her looking at him, smiling with the warmth he had grown to know. Still, he couldn't look at her. He couldn't look at anyone. He wanted to be out among those birds, flying high above himself, this office and all the people below.

Approaching with gentle reassurance, Dr Fallon interrupted the silence. "Orion, I want you to know that I know it's not easy for you to say these things. No one likes to admit that something about them about, which they can't control, has an effect on how people treat them or that the culture with which they identify has deep-rooted prejudices that manifest in, let's say, interesting ways. But I want you to know that the issues we've discussed today are just like every other issue discussed in the past few weeks. They're what?"

Orion couldn't help but smile. Returning from his escape route above the clouds, he could finally look at a human face. "They're solvable."

"That's exactly right," she continued. "You and I are not going to sit here and solve racism nor will we analyse why certain people feel the need to treat you the way you've described. That's their baggage and you will not be carrying it for them. What we're going to do is continue to arm you with the skills and tools to navigate scenarios where you feel trapped so you can better assert your own personality which is something I believe that we all have a right to do."

These optimistic summaries were always Orion's favourite part. In his time with Dr Fallon, he'd been lucky enough to experience three or four. He also tensed himself and dimmed his smile as he had also learned to be weary of speech that seemed like a precursor to hard work on his part.

"Now, we have around ten minutes or so left in the session and I'd like to discuss some exercises that I think would be helpful for you. I also think we should invest in some basic journaling as I feel that would be useful to read out in our next session. The most important thing I want you to do for me though is to try to go out again but this time to a calmer setting. Maybe somewhere social but with a show or act or something. Is there anything that jumps to mind?"

"Actually, there's an open mic poetry reading in KeyTags I was thinking of going to on Thursday night."

"I think that's perfect. I want to see if you can go somewhere without so much scrutiny to conform and hopefully that will ease the pressure we've discussed today. Somewhere where you can maybe reach out to someone or a group over a mutual interest instead of what you can do for one another."

It was over a year ago when Orion had started to write poetry. Long before one bad night out had led him to this blue room. Slowly, he had filled the blank and bare pages of a leather-bound notebook with his imagery, jokes and rhymes. If a human ever had such a thing as a physical and tangible soul, Orion knew his was contained within those pages.

He had never been able to read its contents to anyone. Not once, not to a single living thing. He had long since stopped trying and the upcoming poetry reading would be no exception. "Ya, I could do that. I think you might be right. I probably need to get off the club scene for a while. Try to come out of my shell in different ways. Hopefully I don't blend in with the locals too well and fly too close the sun."

"It's funny, I always think that people so often misinterpret that story."

"Of Icarus?"

"Absolutely. People always refer to it in scenarios where one tries too hard and are let down by their own success but what people forget is that Icarus and his father were imprisoned on the Island of Crete by King Minos. Fashioning wings and trying to escape was his act of defiance. His way of trying to escape the fate that had been laid out for him. Icarus wasn't full of hubris or pride or anything that wasn't perfectly natural. Icarus was just trying to be free, like you."

Green garden and pre-flood majesty hitherto
unknown
A blameless couple in their starter home
A fruit of no import
Out, out forever

The nuclear family gave birth to weaponry
Dominion turned to domination
The seven-day rest begat eternal silence
"Abel", shouted Cain
"I love our parents, but you are pure
I will send your soul to a better place"

The upstairs lounge area of the local queer resource centre filled with finger snaps of appreciation from the crowd. The poem's young composer stood on a small, raised platform. Clutching their small notebook of poetry, they left the stage shortly after receiving an enthusiastic, "Yes, go in poet!" from the crowd.

Orion sat at a small table in the back, his own book of poetry locked safely in a bedside cabinet several miles away. Just as well. Orion's thoughts remained mainly with his most recent session. Looking down at the fizzy drink in his hand, there was a great relief to be socialising somewhere that did not sell alcohol. The mild anti-anxiety medication, to which he had become accustomed over the past few months, did not blend well with a good time. Instead, the cold, sobering fizz produced a not unpleasant caffeine high. Paired pleasantly with poetry and intense introspection.

Naturally, Orion mentally reviewed the talk of the day and, his lack of enthusiasm for the more subtle subtext of Greek mythology aside, he thought it indicated progress. A good day to be sure and so he was content to sit and listen to prose from his fellow amateur poets.

This gap between poets is certainly a bit long, though, he thought.

Perhaps he could do this type of thing more often. Find events around the city that catered to his hobbies.

This silence filling the room is a bit odd. This is a poetry reading, after all. No one in the room has said anything for around fifteen minutes. Maybe even longer.

And then, over time, he might even meet some people. Make some new friends. People to whom he could speak and share and then he wouldn't be alone.

I wonder, has anyone else noticed it? I mean, they must have unless it's on purpose.

That would be nice; people to talk to. Then he wouldn't have to go to therapy. No way. He'd be healthy and happy like everyone else.

Those two guys over there are really cute. I wonder if that child they're with is theirs. That's adorable. I wonder if I'll ever get the chance to have children. I mean, if I was to try, I'd have to be honest with my partner and I'm not sure how they'd react, seeing as I am how I am.

It'd be a shame, Orion thought, to lose Dr Fallon but it would be great to terminate. Plus, if he just worked hard enough, he could even get himself a boyfriend. This was a good day.

This silence is crazy. It's been going on forever. That guy at the table ahead of me keeps looking back. I wonder what he wants? Why is he looking at me? I'm just trying to sit and mind my own business.

Imagine that. A boyfriend. Someone good and kind

and present. I mean, why not? People do it all the time, sometimes by accident and without any effort at all. That's the kind of person Orion could be. This was a good day.

I know what he wants from me. I can see it. Or maybe he's thinking I shouldn't be here. I probably am sticking out a bit. I am the only person in the room at a table on their own. Everyone else has someone with them.

I'd be able to fit in. Today was a good day.

I don't like this. My chest feels tight. I am the only person on their own.

Orion simply needed to relax more. Most people don't need therapy to do that. He could see that now. Today was a good day.

I might need to get out of here. I am the only person on their own.

Today was a good day.

I am the only person on their own.

Alright, fine! I'm here alone; I don't have anyone to come with. I just wanted to sit here and listen to some poetry and now everyone has gone quiet because of me and everyone is probably thinking about me sitting here with my little drink. I don't want to read my poetry, I just want to sit here. The cute guys in the front are probably going to talk about me afterwards and this guy in front of me is probably sharing little glances with his friends. I'm not trying to bother anyone or fit in. I'm just trying to sit here alone but I can't even do that and now everyone just wants me to go so they can get back to the poetry. Well, I have poetry too. I have things to say. Why is everyone so quiet for this long? I don't underst …

Oh no, not again.

A familiar feeling swept over Orion. The room and all its insufferably judgmental occupants seemed far away. An unpleasant sense of a waking dream crept over every surface and face. Both fatigue and excitement gripped Orion and a most unpleasant numbing sensation had appeared behind his eyes. It deeply depressed him that he knew from experience what was soon to follow. Hyperventilating, sweating, a racing heart or just old-fashioned sobbing: Orion didn't know which would come first. He didn't know anything in this moment. He didn't know why this was happening, if anyone could help him or if it would ever stop. The only thing of which he was sure, as he sat alone at a table, enduring the opening savoy of an anxiety attack, was that he needed to be alone right now.

The bathroom's proximity made it the most obvious option. Orion stood up with the intentional finesse of someone trying desperately not to be noticed. Moving slowly and with eyes on the ground, feelings of animosity toward the crowd were stirring in him. As he moved through the densely tabled floor, the next poet ascended the stage and began to recite.

Don't write that, then it will be down on paper
Naked, bare, raw and obvious
A problem recognised but not addressed

Sitting in their small groups, gossiping and whispering. They had absolutely no consideration for how other people felt.

Don't write that, then everyone will know
Out, awkward, distance and pity
An issue spoken but not confessed

Still, Orion wasn't surprised. The selfishness of the average person was a constant source of shock to him.

Don't self-improve, you might fail
Spiral, repetition, relapse and square one
An artist dabbling but not obsessed.

Maybe it wasn't him after all? Ya, that sounded right. More likely that it was the completely empathetic nature of society. Not even these hallowed queer spaces offered a reception for true emotions.

But this epoch is mine
My trans and transient soul deserves confession

No one else had any inkling of personal struggle.

I'm terrified that I might have a drinking problem.

Forty minutes passed. In that time, twelve people came into the bathroom. Orion counted each one. He thought about their day and their lives and whether anyone had noticed a long-term occupant in the last stall, or the previously occupied table back in the recital area.

After a while, these worries passed, and Orion simply split his gaze between the blue, tiled floor and the plain, plaster roof. This was definitely the worst part. The initial physical symptoms of an anxiety attack could maybe be misinterpreted as a precursor to some glorious high. This, however, was a most sobering moment.

Orion sat with his head in his hands attempting to steady his breath, fighting back tears and wondering why this was happening to him. It was clear to him now that nothing had even happened. No calamity had struck or traumatic event transpired. He had simply walked through his day to his destiny: staring at the lines between the tiles in a public bathroom, too afraid to stand up and go home.

Never again, he had thought after his last attack. A clear and determined declaration of improvement. Since then, he had worked out, developed hobbies, met new people and worked out a treatment plan with Dr Fallon. Was all that for nothing? Was the cold and depressingly comforting isolation of a washroom all for which Orion could wish?

Growing bored in the most seductively self-sadistic way possible, Orion's physical body eventually stood up and exited the bathroom. He moved slowly and without a care. What use were cares now? Being out late, his houseplants, work the next day. They all melded in the same swirling, monotonous tunnel of simply existing.

On his exit from the building, Orion paused to stare almost vacantly at the Queer Culture notice board. The room itself was almost empty and it appeared that the poetry reading had ended quite some time ago. Staring at him from the large cork board was a collection of multi-coloured reminders of events to which he felt unwelcome.

A new book club. A jumble sale. Entry information for an upcoming leather and kink pageant. A queer pet grooming service.

So, are the pets groomed in a particularly queer way? Wait! What was that last one?

Orion moved from **Paws for Thought's** flyer to the A4 black and white information for Alt-Kink, 2021.

Alt-Kink, 2021

A pageant of leather, rubber, spandex, latex and all forms of fetish wear, working to display a positive image of the community and the values for which it stands.

Join, discover and decide who you want to be.

Decide who you want to be. Was it that easy? Could Orion simply slap on a harness and some cuffs and suddenly be confident?

The poster went on to provide contact information and a website where more information could be found. Pausing first to make sure no one was looking, Orion snapped a photo and exited, quickly.

On the walk home, he eschewed the headphones in his pocket in place of an unavoidable analysis of the day. Again and again, his thoughts returned to the large A4 poster. Kink and fetish were something in which he had been interested for quite some time but he had always done so as a solitary figure, slowly incorporating elements into his everyday aesthetic. Some boots here or a wrist cuff there. Over time, it had seeped into his motions until it was as unremarkable as other pieces of clothing.

A public event would be very different. He was aware of the Alt-Kink title and knew that the event itself was well attended and usually contained competitors far more experienced than him. That thought was a comfort to Orion. To have enthusiasm and little experience was something awarded less and less as one grew older.

Also, and Orion found this most shocking of all, it actually sounded like fun. Actual, genuine fun. Something of which, he had not had a lot recently.

Orion subtly felt the outline of the phone in his hip pocket. Its digital vaults contained the photo he had taken. More research at home was definitely warranted but as he neared the street on which he lived, the cool evening air proved to be a comfort. The silence which had earlier plagued his day now took the form of a nearly peaceful atmosphere and the dream-like haze was finally beginning to lift.

The worst of the day had passed and, most importantly, there was hope for tomorrow.

Today was a good day.

Chapter 3

Wherein we wished that we lived further away.

(3)

Oh God, what am I going to tell Paulina?

Barry posed the question to himself over and over again. A full workday wasted in thought. Now, it was five thirty in the evening and the sun had already set. Each approaching car shone its dimmed headlights in succession. A kind of rapid light therapy to illuminate one into cognition. No such luck.

Instead, Barry was set to automatic. Wandering through his day in quiet bewilderment, he had completed a full day's work with as little interest as to what was happening around him as possible. This did not, Barry was aware, speak well of any sense of excitement in his profession. His blue uniform, barely creased from a day of inactivity, had long since starched in unison with his life.

Oh God, what am I going to tell Paulina?

On and on it went. The horrible thing was that Barry was no closer to a suitable answer.

Say nothing and abscond to Monaco? No, too expensive and the tax-evader vibe would be a downer.

Send a message and hope the main shock would have subsided by the time he arrived home? Definitely not. A paper trail meant no plausible deniability in the future. No, it had to be face to face.

Stop, have a drink and then scream from the rooftops? Cathartic but chaotic.

God, coming out was such a bore. Why couldn't one skip this initial nerve-wracking bit and just move on to the blanket expressions of love and acceptance? Barry was, after all, just being true to himself and what he wanted.

I'm gay, he thought. *I'm forty-three, I'm married and I'm a gay man.*

Maybe Paulina would approve? Yes, that's the kind of world in which we lived now. Cool urban couples weren't the only weirdos to have marriage dramas worthy of a talk show blowout.

This was unlikely, of course. Paulina lacked Barry's sense of adventure.

God, I wish Paulina was a lesbian. Nothing would make me happier than if I walked in the front door to find my big lesbian wife embroiled in an untoward embrace with another woman. That would solve everything. Even a dalliance with another man would provide beautiful leverage. Why does she have to be so wretchedly in love with me?

Barry's perfect wife. Funny, kind, beautiful and engaging as they come. In the beginning, Paulina's long list of traits had served as reassurance to Barry that he definitely was not gay.

Gay? With a wife like that? Impossible.

Now, Paulina's continued fidelity was a source of guilt and anxiety.

Gay? With a wife like that? Most definitely, and

Barry couldn't even pretend that he wanted to be straight anymore. No self-loathing and no efforts for conversion. Just the mounting feeling that more good years lay behind than ahead.

Was this the initial stages of a mid-life crisis? Had the sexual lifestyle change replaced the more classic face lift and second-hand Ferrari?

Oh God, what am I going to tell Paulina?

Barry tightened his grip on the black leather steering wheel. Looking to escape the frantic question in his mind, he thought back to his most recent venture out. Walking into that nightclub, he had taken pleasure in his anonymity. He wasn't a husband or a worker. He was barely even a citizen. He was just another customer looking to enjoy himself.

His early trips out had been an exercise in people watching. Slowly, he came to identify the different sets of people. Granted, some parts still eluded him and those young gender-liquid people, or whatever they called themselves, were a bit intense for his liking.

Only three times had he built up the nerve to try some flirting. The first did not go well. As far as Barry could remember, the guy to which he was speaking turned and walked away somewhere during Barry's ten-minute speech on the current complexities of the housing market. By the second time he had learned to relax and listen. This, coupled with his more disposable income than the average patron, proved successful. So, one Friday night on the second floor of a crowded nightclub that seemed to vibrate and breath in its own right, Barry broke his wedding vows for the first time.

Months had passed since that night and short of inventing time travel, there was nothing to be done. All Barry could do now was cut his losses (a blissful marriage of twelve years) and await some well-earned kudos for his bravery.

Running into Jamie on his most recent night out was a nice surprise, as was the large black guy he was with. Barry loved black guys. So strong and masculine.

After leaving them, he had spent the night talking to Stephen, a slim man in his thirties. The top three buttons of his shirt were open to reveal a muscular and well-cologned chest. After an hour or so, Stephen gave him his number. Barry entered it into his phone as 'Stephen work' and headed home to Paulina.

Barry loosened his grip on the wheel. His sweating palms were making steering a hazardous endeavour. Maybe a nice car crash would be in order? Take a swerve and confess to his wife while in the sympathy cocoon of a full body cast.

No, Barry. Think of the insurance premiums.

Home was closer now. Another ten minutes or so and he would have to explain the whole ugly affair (although obviously not the actual ugly affair part).

Maybe Barry could simply keep driving?

Even better, abandon the car, rip the uniform from his body and hear the satisfying crush of his phone under his naked heel. Barry imagined walking from this quiet suburban street only to emerge somewhere else with a new life. No memories of confession or betrayal. No memories at all, if that was an option. Bearded and living under a new name, he would live cursed with the beautiful burden of freedom.

Just a thought, of course. They'd find him eventually. They always do. What kind of modern society was this where a man can't even leave his loved ones and live under an assumed identity in a foreign land? It's PC culture gone mad.

Oh God, what am I going to tell Paulina?

Well, now was the time to find out. The sight of Barry's, red-brick house came into view as he turned the corner onto his silent cul-de-sac. Fighting the very strong urge to say nothing and spend the night in quiet resentment, Barry armed himself with resolve before exiting his car and entering through the front door of his home.

Hearing instrumental music intruding from the living room, Barry knew that he had walked in on Paulina's reading time.

Oh, great. My embarrassment will have a soundtrack, he thought. *How appropriately undermining.*

"B, is that you?"

Presence detected. The opportunity to disappear without a trace had officially passed.

"Ya, P. I'm home."

Walking into the living room, Paulina was curled up on a leather armchair reading some ghastly true-crime book and nursing a half glass of Sauvignon Blanc. Her blond hair, tied back in a ponytail, was peeking out at the front to meet the rims of her reading glasses. Looking up from some serial killer's confession, she smiled with great warmth.

"Hey, you. How was work?"

How was work? What kind of question was that? Work was work. What a leading question from Lady Columbo. Did she know? Was that it? Perhaps he was as easy to read as one of her books. If that was the case, Barry would have to think of an original response to this interrogation.

"Work was fine. A bit long but it's over now."

Oh, genius. What incredible powers of evasion and subterfuge. It was good to know that if he was ever captured by enemy troops, they wouldn't need to resort to torture to exhaust his mental dexterity. God, this was awful. Barry knew he needed a moment in which to interject. Some opportunity to naturally move the conversation, so much as it was one, toward his confession. Just one seamless transition.

"I suppose so," Paulina began. "Today did seem long. I thought it felt like a Tues"

"I'M GAY!" shouted Barry with the seamless tact for which he was known. Sitting down next to Paulina, he took her free hand in his.

"I'm sorry for interrupting but I really am quite gay."

The expression on her face and in her eyes was not one of shock but compassion. Placing her book on the ground, she joined her hands together around Barry's. "Yes, I know, we've spoken about this before."

51

"I know, I know, I know, but this is different. When I came out to you last year, I was just telling you how I felt. You took it super well and I really do love you for that."

"And this is different somehow?" she asked.

"Yes, different. I've been thinking recently and now I'm pretty clear as to what I want."

They had, throughout their marriage, had many revealing conversations. The death of her father. Barry's first coming out. The purchase of a domestic water heater had once led to a two-hour debate about the afterlife. He wanted to say it, but the words wouldn't come. Still no answer to his day-long question.

"Are you going to tell me, or shall we play gay charades?" she asked.

Now or never and never wasn't really an option.

"I think I want to start pursuing a gay lifestyle and I can't do that if I'm living like the straight guy I was trying to be. He doesn't exist. He has no life."

The compassion had long since drained from her face. Taking her hands from his, she reached down for a gulp of wine from her glass.

Nursing no more.

"Are you saying this to me because you have done something you shouldn't have?" she asked.

"No, of course not."

He was.

Sounding unconvinced, Paulina could not look at her husband's face. "And do you still have romantic feelings for me?"

"Of course, I do."

He didn't.

"Look, P, I know this is weird but it's definitely not out of the blue. It's difficult for me too."

"Difficult!" she repeated with barely contained venom. "This is not just difficult for me. I feel completely blindsided. Ten minutes ago, I was sitting in the house we own together reading a book. Now, my husband of twelve years is telling me that he wants to leave and start a vegan bakery in San Francisco. How do you think I'm supposed to react? You know, when you came out to me, I was shocked but also happy because I knew how great you must have felt finally saying it. I knew you had held that inside for God knows how long. Now you're coming to me with another little secret and I bet you enjoyed keeping it to yourself until now. Just a little bit. So brilliant and clever you were keeping this from the old wife. What an achievement! You know, I hope you're happy because it doesn't matter how difficult you feel this is, at least you're making a decision. You're driving this horrible situation. I'm just a participant in the Barry show, as usual."

Standing up from her chair, she downed the remaining contents of the glass and walked over to stare at the wall above the fireplace. Barry looked at her and continued his day-long indulgence of wondering what to say. Suddenly, he was back at their wedding day. Barry had caught a glimpse of her from behind before the ceremony. She was radiant and beautiful. Gay or not, he loved her so much that day. After that, he had spent time alone trying to think of some words of adoration. Words about how she had saved him. Words about how he loved her. Words about how he would always be true. Where were those words and promises now when he needed them most?

"P," began Barry, "I just feel like I—"

"Oh, of course! Tell me how you feel. I'm absolutely dying to know your feelings. We all have to do what we feel all the time? This is the real world, Barry. We don't always get to be who we want." She reached over and grabbed a framed photo from atop the fireplace. "You told me you understood that when you made a commitment to staying for me and the kids."

Holding out the photo of her family like a shield, Barry looked back to that day at the international Down syndrome family fun day. A friend of theirs had suggested bringing four-year-old Kevin to meet other children. Caroline, ever the supportive older sister of two years, was excited to be brought along too. Paulina adored the picture, so she had it framed and placed on the mantel where it had waited for a year to be used as a prop in this facile interchange between husband and wife.

Barry hated that photo. The bright and hopeful eyes of his two children looked up at him from the past, completely unaware of the emotional blackmail their presence would invoke.

"Oh, the kids, the kids, the kids! You're acting like I haven't thought of them once."

"Well, have you?" she asked, returning the photo to

the mantelpiece. "Because we are their parents, Barry. We all love each other, and we live in a house and we share our lives. That's what we've given them their entire lives. Last year you said you wanted to continue that. What happened to that?"

"Nothing happened, Paulina. The kids are fine. You can't keep acting like they're made of glass and will grow up to be criminals if we don't continue this Norman Rockwell lie that we've been feeding them." Both Barry and Paulina were on their feet now. The instrumental music continued to play on in the background. "And don't think I haven't noticed that you've amped up the parent sympathy stuff in the past year."

"What are you talking about?" she asked.

"Oh, Barry, Caroline and Kevin said the funniest thing today when you were away. Oh, Barry, the kids were saying how much they love it when you tuck them in at night. Oh, Barry, the kids said they love it when we get to have a family dinner together. It's pathetic!"

Paulina stood, mouth slightly agape. Barry was immediately aware that he may have crossed a line.

"They're our children, you psychopath! Most fathers don't view updates of their children's lives as an inconvenience, you cowardly, cruel, worm!"

"I'm not most fathers, Paulina, and all the name calling in the world won't change that. Now, whether you like it or not, I'm a grown man and I decide how I live. If this were a different time, I could have just saddled up a horse and slipped away in the night."

"Are you seriously expecting me to thank you for

not abandoning your family in some equine-themed bid for freedom?"

"Of course not," said Barry, choosing to forget his earlier thoughts. If he couldn't remember them, she couldn't force them out of him. "I just want you to know that I have be able to decide my own life."

"It's not just your life anymore, Barry. It's our life now. We built this together. You made commitments to me and then we had children, for God's sake. Plus, throughout all that, all you've ever done is what you wanted. You had a selfish streak in you going back to day one."

"I am not selfish," said Barry, selfishly.

"Would you keep your voice down," said Paulina, loudly.

"This is exactly what I'm talking about! I'm not even shouting and you ask me to keep it down. Don't shout, don't talk, don't feel. You're running my life like some sort of Victorian asylum. And keep my voice down for who? The kids? The kids can't hear us. None of this is hurting them. They won't explode if they're not raised exactly like the majority of their friends."

The conversation had reached an apex. Both parties knew it. To avoid any accusations of physical intimidation, Barry sat down. Paulina, who had turned back toward the fireplace, eventually walked toward her chair, retrieved a remote and switched off her reading music.

"Barry," she asked, "is there someone else?"

A fair question given the circumstances but also a

question to which Barry could give an honest answer. "There's no one else, Paulina." Honest, if you discount his earlier dalliance and lovely Stephen of course. "But there could be, you know. There's no one now but I think I deserve to see if there might be in the future."

"That's all hypothetical though, B. You might have someone in the future. I'm right here. I'm here now, I love you and I'm the mother of your children." She spoke with a tone of genuine hopefulness as if she could find the right combination of words to break this gay spell. Barry found it exhausting. This whole situation was exhausting.

Looking around the room, he could count five different pictures of himself and his family. Happy scenarios that had led him to this conversation. Part of him wanted to mentally airbrush himself from those photos like some gay, Stalinist purge of memory. To continue to pursue his claim was to invite a long night of name calling, tension and the dogged sponsorship of his own free will.

"I'm sure if you think about it for a few days, you'll see what I'm saying and make the right choices," she insisted.

Was this even a choice anymore? Barry honestly couldn't tell. The part of his brain that processed different outcomes based on his actions, had been eroded from a day of worrying. Choosing was a mental capacity beyond him at this moment. How terribly convenient. Instead, he let his lower brain function take over and endeavoured to end this conversation and return to a place of manageable contentedness as soon as possible.

"Okay, maybe we should table this for another time. I came in here pretty hot and I think you might be right; I am being a bit selfish. Okay?"

"I think that's best," she said, sliding her hand back onto his – the not-so-subtle Pavlovian response that indicated she approved of what Barry was saying. "This has been a lot so I'm going to check on the kids and then turn in. You coming up?"

"Sure thing. I'll be up soon."

His wife. His jail warden. His opponent. She had grown to be all these things to him. Slowly, she retrieved her long-empty glass and book before walking quietly toward the door.

"I love you, Barry," she said before exiting.

"I love you too, Paulina," was his response. What was another lie among a foundation?

Time to rationalise why this wasn't a complete and utter failure, thought Barry. *Completely chickening out could be part of my long-term master plan. By this rate, I should be out of this house by my sixties.*

Barry sat with similar thoughts for over an hour. While he did so, the noise of the house continued. The dishwasher laboured to erase any hint that a good meal had ever been enjoyed. Paulina's shower from upstairs hummed and buzzed while it both soothed and scolded. The dripping of a nearby tap was a homely metronome keeping track of time slipping inexorably away.

Barry hated all of it.

No, it was more than hate. At that moment, Barry

despised every pipe, corner, pillow, plate and wall in his own home. The television, the toaster and the tea towels were his enemies, every vase and vacuum were his captors and every single one of those perfectly placed pictures were his overseers.

This night was supposed to end differently. He was hoping to set himself up for the night on the very couch upon which he currently sat. He had, in his day-long planning, even chosen a blanket and pillow combination.

What was this place? How did he come to be here?

Some men were banished to the lonely Elba Island of the downstairs couch for minor marital infractions. Barry had made a genuine attempt to leave his wife and now, only an hour or so later, he was expected to share her bed. What strange tendrils of desperation had grabbed hold of their marriage, grown from some festering mega-plant of fear? How odd that he should desire nothing more than retribution against him. To be kicked out and asked not to return. No body part was quite so desirable as that of a cold shoulder. No embrace more pleasurable than that of a hug goodbye.

Rising from the couch and ascending the stairs, Barry looked down the hall toward the slightly ajar door of Kevin and Caroline's room. Peeking inside, he could see them both in their beds, sleeping gently. Caroline's blond hair was so much like her mother's.

Looking around their room, he could feel his temper cool. Barry did not despise his children and as an extension, he did not feel trapped when looking at them. Drawings of silly creatures and castles adorned their walls. Barry moved quietly into the room to meet a picture Kevin had drawn and placed over his bed. Onto its blank, white surface, he had drawn green grass, a blue sky, a pointy house and a standing family of four.

My God, are they all in on it? Will he greet me tomorrow morning with a fresh "Don't go, Daddy" tattoo on his little arm?

The cartoon figure representing him stood at the beginning of the line, holding Paulina's cartoon hand. She, in turn, held Caroline who held Kevin. This meant that in the line, Kevin, the artist of this piece, had placed himself as far from Barry as possible. This did not go unnoticed, but Barry would ruminate on it later. Right now, he just looked at his cartoon persona and knew that the broad, if not slightly uneven, smile on his face was a lie. It was drawn on by a child of four with no concept of regret.

Barry wondered how they would draw him after. Would they sketch and paint images of their father with admiration or disdain? Would he still hold hands in unison with the family and enjoy the colourful splendour of that green grass and blue sky? Barry would never leave his children. Or at the very least, he did not want to. Of course, deep down, he knew that he didn't even want, really want, to leave Paulina. Why would he do that when she had been nothing but a supportive and nurturing partner and mother for several years? No, Barry knew the truth.

Barry wanted to leave himself. Part of him hated himself. The past he had amassed was one of corrosive, selfish convention. He knew that rebirth was also an act of murder, but he never was one for the lamentation of regrets.

A mercy killing, he assured himself.

The time was late. As usual he was the last one awake in the house but now his half of the marriage bed beckoned. At the end of a long day, Barry stripped away his starched blue uniform, but had been unable to soften the stiffness in himself. Instead, breaking the golden rule of never going to bed mad, he climbed in between the sheets and beside Paula. This was only the latest in his long line of marriage violations.

Selfish, thought Barry. *That's what she called me. Me, of all people. Everything I've done has been for other people. How can having a miserable father and husband be good for anyone? No, I'm definitely in the right. I mean, this way, Paulina can still find someone else and the kids are still young enough to adapt to a new home life. It's perfect but I can't do anything until they see that what's good for me is good for the family.*

I wonder if I should call and see if I can meet up with Stephen tomorrow? Or text or app or whatever. I liked him a lot and he seemed nice. I suppose, given today, I should probably come home tomorrow after work. Actually, this is important, and I deserve it after what I've been through. Paulina won't mind.

Actually, she definitely won't mind because I have no intention of telling her.

Free Like You

Chapter 4

Wherein we wish
that we were an
inanimate object
with stylish
curves.

(4)

She's pregnant

Jamie 15:34

Who?

Akib 15:34

Caoimhe

Jamie 15:35

Caoimhe?

Akib 15:35

Yesum

Jamie 15:36

Who in this glittering galaxy is Caoimhe?

Akib 15:38

She's the girl I went home with three weeks ago when we were out.

Jamie 15:40

The girl you went home with"?

Was that before your job on the construction site or after you were searching car lots for a second-hand BMW?

Akib 15:44

Ya I made the jump to hetero.
Very funny

Do you remember three weeks ago, we were out and I brought that person with dark hair back to our table and then we danced and then left together?

Jamie 15:47

THAT'S what you did after you left together? I thought you were going to an after party or going to find Buy-a-Bag Barry.

Akib 15:51

We grabbed a cab back to hers and one thing led to another

Jamie 15:55

One thing led to another?

Like, who is this?

Is this still Jamie?

You sound like you're messaging from a Judd Apatow film.

Akib: 15:59

Stop, Akib, I'm serious. She's pregnant. She just called me

Jamie 16:01

I mean, are you sure that it's yours?
Do you even remember what you did?

Akib: 16:05

I'm not sure

Jamie 16:05

You're not sure?

Akib: 16:07

Okay, I remember perfectly. It's seared into my little brain.

Jamie: 16:09

Wow. So how was it?

Akib: 16:10

It was actually great but my recollection is becoming tainted by this growing sensation of anxiety and shame.

What is this feeling?

Jamie: 16:13

I think the heteros call it guilt

Akib: 16:14

Oh, I've heard of that. Like when you buy a Jeffree Starr pallet

Jamie: 16:14

So, what happened?

Akib: 16:15

It's just really well made, and I guess my eyes got the better of me. I hide it when people come over though.

Jamie: 16:17

I mean with Caoimhe

Akib: 16:20

Oh, right. Ya she called me and told me. At first I thought she was joking. She said that she hadn't been with someone for a while before me and no one since then so I'm the lucky daddy

Jamie: 16:26

God that looks so wrong

Akib: 16:28

I know. It looked wrong as soon as I typed it

Jamie: 16:33

You're the least daddy person I know

Akib: 16:33

Now you can never say that again. I got someone pregnant and on the first time, too! All that time batting my eyelashes and cropping tops for free drinks. I should have just been selling my super sperm

Akib, am I a superman?

Jamie: 16:37

Ya I remember reading that one where Superman styles a wig faster than a speeding bullet.

Akib: 16:40

Oh god, this is all way too real. It's not fair. I didn't know what I was doing. I just used context clues and made a few educated guesses.

This is the most perverse participation trophy I could imagine.

Jamie: 16:43

So, Jamie you great big procreator, what are you going to do? By which I mean, of course, how does Caoimhe want to handle this?

Akib: 16:46

She wants to keep it

Jamie: 16:50

Please tell me by "it" you mean her freedom

Akib: 16:51

She explained it on the phone and it's complex and I can't really go through it here

Jamie: 16:52

You want to come over?

Akib: 16:54

Yes

Jamie: 16:54

You want to grab two bottles of wine on the way?

Akib: 16:55

Double Yes

Jamie: 16:55

*****

Forty minutes later, Jamie sat, cross-legged, on one of the many eclectic and reclaimed pieces of furniture strewn throughout Akib's tattered and homely apartment. A colourful nest of charity shop bizarreness, it was situated on the sixth floor of a worn and broken-bricked building in an erstwhile industrial area of town. The pink and blinding light of a dying day filled the room as Akib filled two odd gin glasses with the contents of one of Jamie's bottles.

"At least you aren't the one who'll have to give up drinking," said Akib while handing Jamie half a bottle's worth.

"Ya, thank god for small miracles."

"Speaking of small miracles, what the hell happened, sis?"

"I don't know," Jamie answered, using their acrylics to tap the side of the now partly emptied glass. "Something just happened, and we were all out and well you were there. You saw her."

"Ya, I saw her; I didn't impregnate her. I mean, this is bath bomb bizarre. I wouldn't have even thought that you'd be able."

"Biology can be very cruel, I guess."

"God, I wish you had told me that before I transitioned. Plus, after that scare with Hairy Back a year ago, I thought you always insisted on safe play, no matter what the scenario."

"I do!" Jamie exclaimed. "Or I thought I did. This is totally unfair and not what I was promised."

"Promised?"

"Promised!" Jamie stood to their feet, downed another mouthful of problem-solving miracle juice and gesticulated to Akib with their free hand. "I could never throw a ball or hang out with the boys growing up and the older I got, the worst it got, like when they tried to make you wear dresses when you were little."

"It's funny because I love wearing dresses now."

"We both love it now, but it was hard sometimes growing up and all that was fine because I knew that I was fabulous. One hundred percent caret gold, diamond-coated fabulousness. I was the queer kid which meant I was an alien with this whole other world to explore. I knew it was my reward because I had earned it. That's what was promised to me – but this? This doesn't even make sense. I'm going to be a father now? Seriously, sis, what even is that? What was the point of all the name calling and bullying growing up if I was just going to end up here?"

Jamie downed yet another mouthful of the, <u>totally not in any way contributing to their problems,</u> content of their glass and looked across the scattered room to a tailor's dummy which Akib had affectionately named Oubliette. On Oubliette's face, Akin had placed a small mirror. Looking into that mirror, just for a second, Jamie could see their face atop those desirable and stylish curves. This was where Jamie wanted to be. Beloved, revered and as much a fashion icon as one could hope to be. Standing upright, they would not fret or opine on important issues. Their only opinions would be toward the new outfit they helped create and the promise it was designed to fulfil.

"So, are we going to discuss the ugliness?" asked Akib.

"The ugliness?"

"Ya, you know. The ugly question."

Jamie shrugged. Akib sighed in response. "The ugly subject of keeping the little one."

"Oh! There's nothing ugly about a person's right to choose, Akib."

"Oh, don't front that one with me, honey. I was marching and campaigning for a person's right to choose before we even met. Remember when I campaigned our school to start a reproductive rights club and wouldn't show up to class for a week in protest when they refused?"

"Why did you eventually show up to class again?"

"Because an education, my skinny friend, is important."

"Hard to deny that. I mean, look how far it's gotten you. Bt-dubz, is that a new wig?"

"Yes, girl, it is!" Akib extended their leg blatant and upright like the flashing feline they were before standing up and walking to a long, red head of hair resting across the room on one the apartment's many Styrofoam busts. "I forget to mention it with the whole, your like falling apart, thing but it arrived yesterday."

Akib ran their hand through red majesty, their long fingers gliding easily through the already styled waves. "I call her …" Akib looked away and then back toward Jamie with their best dramatic flair, "Cassundra!"

All Jamie could do was groan and fall, crumpled, into Akib's bed, making sure to keep their glass and its contents safe.

"You don't like my Cassy?" asked Akib.

"Of course I do, she's everything, but I'm so screwed that I can't even appreciate a new look. I probably wouldn't even notice if you slapped me across the face with some Louis Vuittons."

"If I had some Vuittons, the last thing I'd do is slap them against your busted old mug," said Akib as they moved from Cassundra back to one of their perfectly imperfect chairs. "So, tell me, where are we when it comes to a termination?"

"Hurfiftheradun," said Jamie, face buried in a pillow.

"One more time, sis."

"Her sister had one," said Jamie as they turned around to stare at the ceiling. "A few years ago, her sister had an abortion and apparently it was more traumatic for her than she thought. Caoimhe wasn't too heavy on the details but she said she never wanted to go through that. I told her what I thought, of course, that an ethical, medically sound termination doesn't have to be this huge traumatic thing and that she didn't have to be burdened with any negative feelings."

"Wowsers. So, what did she say?"

"She said that she had thought about it and that it was her choice and that she had made it." Jamie continued to stare at the bedroom's pink plaster ceiling until they heard Akib screw the metal cap from the second bottle of wine and begin to pour.

"No offence but Caoimhe sounds like an absolute boss."

"I'm glad you're enjoying this."

"I'm sorry but she does," said Akib, moving from their glass to Jamie's. "That had to be a tough call to make. Plus, here's you who's been pro-choice since you were able to speak and now look where you are. Is that irony?"

"I'm way too queer, upset and drunk to have an opinion."

"Stop thinking of names for your biography and calm down. Have another drink."

Jamie followed the latter suggestion but not the former.

"So, what does this mean for you and Caoimhe?"

All of a sudden, Jamie was forty-three years old. Their passionless labour, derived from necessity and the hungry, gnashing mouths of responsibility, allowed them no respite. They lived with quiet resentment toward their wife of twenty years. The needs and wants of their parasitic offspring subconsciously consumed their every waking hour and reverberated forward to an economic coffin and back to the youthful figure staring at the pink ceiling in a post-bohemian style apartment.

"No," said Jamie aloud.

"No?"

"I don't know what this means for myself and Caoimhe." This was the truth. Jamie had spoken to Caoimhe only a few hours ago and during the entire conversation, she never once indicated what it was she wanted from them. No expectation of support, assistance or even presence. This was as anxiety inducing as it was perplexing. "Oh God, what if she wants me to propose or move in or something?"

"I mean, it's defo not outside the realms of possibility. You do share at least some of the responsibility for this situation."

"Don't refer to my child as a situation."

Akib visibly winced. "Ya, it's a deal as long as you don't say the word child until at least the late trimester."

Shall we consider that a new C word?

"Well, now that I know how fond you are of the other one."

Jamie laughed for the first time today. A loud laugh of shrieking abandon that only Akib could help induce. "Ugh, maybe I should just propose. Get down on one knee, get a job in some factory somewhere and try to carve out some happiness."

"They might give you a slimming jumpsuit. Berlin, industrial chic. You might have to trade that open toe for a steel one."

"I'm serious, sis. I could just go full in. Marry Caoimhe, raise the little life-ruiner and teach them everything I know."

"Jamie, you drunken twinkster, we're not even twenty years old. We're barely supposed to know things, let alone teach them to kids. We're only children ourselves. Speaking of which, what are you going to tell your parents?"

Their parents? How could Jamie not have thought of them once over the last few hours? Too occupied, Jamie surmised, with the prospect of a hungry, juvenile mouth eating their future. What would Ted and Moira think? Blanket support was all Jamie could imagine. Their parents had always been good that way. Never shy or ashamed of their youngest child. While some of Jamie's friends would occasionally speak of being cast out of home after a melodramatic coming-out scene, Jamie would think back to the eve of their departure to the big city when their mother was practically grabbing their arm in an attempt to keep them in the company of family. Jamie always thought it was because she was scared of what would happen to them in the real world.

This scenario, Jamie surmised, is definitely not what she expected.

Jamie's parents had, over the past two years, tried to give them money and parental guidance. They had accepted the latter always, but never the former as they saw the offer of monetary assistance for what it was: fear. Hope also, but mainly fear. Jamie had, a long time ago, made it their mission to make their own way in life and expunge their parent's fear. Plus, they preferred the hustle that a cash strapped early adulthood invited.

"My parents will probably be fine. I mean, you know how they are. They'll probably offer me free babysitting and my own au pair if I come home."

"After the initial confusion, of course."

"Oh, there will definitely be some initial confusion."

That was an understatement as far as Jamie was concerned. They had, over the course of their short life, seen fit to drop one or two pieces of information on their parents that might indicate a lifestyle which was different to what they had both envisioned. A baby, however, which was neither miraculous nor charitably procured, would undoubtedly be the most difficult to explain.

Jamie could only imagine how the conversation would go. The awkward summoning of parties, the jilted opening remarks, the brief as possible explanation of events and finally, the relentlessly positive focus on the future. Actually, the more Jamie thought, the more the hypothetical conversation took on a familiar formula.

"Oh God, I'm going to have to come out to my parents again!"

Akib almost rolled from their chair in laughter. Jamie could only turn, present their back to the pink plastered wall, and bury their face in a garishly multi-coloured pillow. "No, no, no! I've done it already! Twice! This isn't fair. I mean, Mother, Father, I'm a procreator. How will that go down?"

"Knowing your parents, they'll probably buy you a house and set up a trust fund."

"I'm going to feel like I'm twelve again. Trembling and scared to come out the first time. It's so … pedestrian. John Waters always said that coming out was so square." Jamie turned and faced Akib, their only hope. "What did you do? Like, all the times you came out. How many was it again?"

"Technically," began Akib, "it was five times but by the third time, it was just me updating her on where I was and how I was developing. Mom handled it all pretty well. When I was eleven, I came out as gay and that was okay because it was 2011 and it wasn't that uncommon especially among girls, so I think Mom was okay with a little, cute lesbian daughter. Then, when I was fifteen, I came out as trans. As you can imagine, that was a rough one. Mom was supportive but I got the usual stuff. Asking me how I could be sure at such a young age and all that. But, after I sat her down and we talked, she came around. A year or so later, I came out as bi and I remember she honestly never even put down her newspaper. She just looked at me from over the page, told me that was good, that she loved me and asked me where I wanted to go for dinner that night. Then, eventually, I came out as pansexual. That one was odd only because it required a bit of explaining on my part, but I was seventeen, so I had a pretty good grip on things. Finally, I came out as gender-fluid. Now that was a messy one because with my preference for pronouns, it required a conscious effort on her part. Also, she had a few minutes where she thought that I wasn't trans anymore and the transition had been a mistake. I explained to her how that wasn't true, and I appreciated all her support. So ya, I would say that I have a pretty decent idea of what I'm doing."

"So out of all those, which one seems to affect you most on a day-to-day basis?"

"Hard to say. Obviously, I'm all of that and so much more every minute of the live-long day but I suppose being a person who's trans probably comes up the most but sometimes in strange ways. Lately, I've been getting a lot of *actually attractive.*"

"What's an actually attractive?" asked Jamie.

"It's this thing where someone, usually a guy, just learns that you're a person who's trans and at some point they come up to you and tell you that <u>actually</u>, they find you very attractive anyway. Then they just smile like they're waiting for some Noble Prize for daring to cross this great cultural chasm. It's embarrassing and only leads to hurt feelings when you turn them down because they have this entitled attitude like I should be grateful for their attention."

"Men are trash."

"Most definitely but it's not always men. Plus, it's not all bad, sometimes I experience the old trans switcheroo which is where I tell someone that I'm a person who's trans and they say something like, *oh, so you want to transition into a woman*, and I just laugh."

Jamie just stared at their best friend and every Pride tattoo that was inked with brazen permanency into their skin. They loved them so much. "I've heard you tell that story before, but I adore it more each time."

"I know you do," said Akib. "That's why I love you, babe."

"So, do you have any more coming out planned?"

Akib bit their lower lip and stared to the side. "I've been vegan for a while now. Might be a good opportunity to make a scene at Christmas."

"Do have any advice for me?" asked Jamie.

"Nope."

"Nope?"

"That's what I said. I mean, you know what you

have to do. It's not emotional. It's practical. You just have to go home, get them together and tell them what happened. After some initial shock, they will understand and probably handle it a bit better than you are. They've been through it all before, after all. Kids, pregnancy, even telling their own parents. This is your future and Moira and Ted will want to be involved."

That was the future that lay ahead. Endless sympathy, supportive family and comforts aplenty. Christ, it sounded awful. Jamie was many things, but they never thought of themselves as fundamentally guilty. To the contrary, anything they had done, they had paid for with gusto and great personal satisfaction. Every hardship and its associated degradation was a welcome and cherished step on the road to being themselves.

This punishment, however, seemed disproportionate with the crime. The sentence too long and the price too steep for the corresponding pleasure. What grand jury had decided this? Jamie was to suffer for all time in the warm, suburban-soaked cardigan of financed parenthood because they took something that perhaps was not theirs to take?

"What if I don't want it to be my future, sis?" they asked.

"A bit too late for that, stud. I'm afraid you've gone and charmed your way into a life sentence."

Jamie raised the glass to their glossy lips and downed another mouthful. What recourse did they have now but to drink? One should always waste time that they don't have and this was definitely an example of precious time slipping away. Jamie thought for a moment and pictured the future.

Pictured their child.

A more perverse and unnatural fantasy Jamie could not fathom. They had never wanted children. Never even entertained the idea.

"Do you think queer people should have children?" Jamie knew they had phrased the question incorrectly as soon as they heard it. Akib's face provided additional evidence. "No, I don't mean it like that. Well, actually, I dunno. It's just ... listen, we're young but we've been around and seen stuff. Every ball and rave and art exhibit and festival, and pretty much during none of that time did I think it was a lifestyle for child rearing. Do you remember Celestine who lived on Dawson?"

"Remember? I fell in love with them every time I saw them. I literally wept when they walked the runway at the Dark Fantasy Ball."

"OMG same! It was sickening and transcendent. Celestine was an absolute idol. They walked and talked queer culture. I mean they made even you look like Ronald Reagan. They didn't take any BS from anyone and they were always able to look after themselves. I always thought they were so cool, even after they passed. More than aesthetic goals. Spirit goals. After life goals."

"And you don't think they would have made a good parent?" asked Akib.

"I mean, do you? Celestine was an absolute icon. I idolised them but after the work and the charity and the independence and the looks, I would still have to say no.

They died as they lived. Absolutely sickening and with no apologies or regrets but I still can't make the jump in my brain and if I don't think that someone I absolutely idolised would have made parent, what hope is there for me? I mean, I know that the cloned, preference-gays can settle down in the burbs and talk about their mutual distrust of the homeless but that's not me. I'm a filthy queer superhero and I love it. I never wanted to be anything different."

Jamie wasn't sure if they had lost some of Akib's respect. It was impossible to tell. When they wanted, those big brown eyes gave away nothing. Instead, Jamie just looked to the side as Akib downed a small sip from their glass. Jamie knew better than to say any more. Just stare blankly at the ceiling and pretend like they weren't waiting for Akib to speak.

"I mean, I think you're wrong but I'm not the one having the little ball of cells. "Plus," continued Akib, adopting a cheerier tone, "you've completely neglected the idea of spite."

"Spite? What place would spite have in child rearing? That's what divorces were for."

"I mean, we're in this great queer culture and the one thing that the others had over us was that we couldn't have kids and infect them with our perverted ideas of gender equality and artistic therapy. The idea absolutely terrified them. Even some of our more passable gay comrades were confused as to how anyone could make a family outside their explosive nuclear setup. Now, we can do just that." Akib placed their now empty glass on the ground and held up their hands so as to better illustrate their vision. "Imagine a world of scene queens, runway icons, outside artists, lather freaks and gentle, free love trail heads all armed with kids. We could show the world a better way or at the very least, a new way that's just as good. We could send them out into the world as secret agents, slowly infecting society until the freak flag flies in every country. Frankly, I won't be happy until world leaders are discussing their problems in the queer and crowded wings of a Francis Bacon art exhibit."

"Maybe they could just take it out on the runway and winner takes all?"

"Competition is inherently corrosive, sis. You know that. Still, you could be the first one. You could bring the little so and so to the top of the mountain like Simba and show him off for the cheering primates underneath."

Jamie, whose head was now actually beginning to hurt, could only take one more sip and hope it would help them take in any of whatever Akib was saying. "You know, you get way more abstract the more you drink."

"I know," said Akib through a perfect smile, "and I love you for noticing."

Jamie appreciated that Akib was trying. It had always been each other's responsibility to distract the other until the hard times passed but the current conundrum boasted no expiration date. There would be no relief. No respite for our fabulous protagonist. So, with that in mind, Jamie set aside their now empty glass and asked the one question to which they had been leading all evening. "How much do you think my life is going to change?"

It was a very fair question as far as Jamie was concerned. Obviously, they knew the situation stretched out far beyond their needs (that's why they weren't borrowing money from Akib for the first flight out of the country), but Jamie also knew that they liked their life. The pursuit, the struggle, the adoration, and the friends they had accumulated all made for a lifestyle which, up to a few hours ago, had provided ample contentment. It was natural to want to hold onto that happiness.

"I mean, do you think I'll still be able to go out with you and everyone? Get trade? Guess where Ren is from?"

Akib looked at their best friend without responding for as long as they could before moving down from their chair to sit, cross-legged on the floor. "Sis, come here."

"No, come on, no. Just tell me, please."

"I'll tell you anything you want, just come here."

Tears were forming now in Jamie's blue eyes. A perfect match to their trembling bottom lip. They climbed from the bed down to the floor, lay spread out on the baroque rug and lay their head right in Akib's lap. Akib, always attuned to the physical needs of a situation, gently brushed the short mound of hair on Jamie's head and held Jamie's hand in theirs.

"I'm not going to lie; this is going to be rough for you. I've known you most of your life and I know this wasn't part of your plan. I'd love to tell you that everything will be fine or that this will blow over, but I really don't know anything about what you're going through. You've finally wandered into unchartered territory, but I want you to know that I will be going with you every step of the way. I won't let you do this by yourself." Akib moved their hand to wipe a mascara-infused tear from Jamie's face. "I won't let you do this alone."

Jamie simply laid there for what seemed like a long time, feeling Akib's hand run through their hair and the unashamed tears of lost youth roll down their cheeks. They appreciated everything that Akib was doing but they knew the truth: they had messed up. There was no denying it. They had finally gone too far and now where they were going, not even Akib could follow. So, the two just sat there on that oddly carpeted floor for a while, hands intertwined but undeniably separated by a razor thin filament that divided one person, filled with sympathy, and another who was just very scared of the future.

A few hours at Akib's place and the accompanying bottle of wine made for a strange walk home. All the sights, once so familiar to Jamie, seemed distant. The sun had long set and so Jamie walked through the dark and abandoned alleys of the former industrial estate. Rough and random items were strewn along the streets. Bricks, tubing and random sheets of metal. Looking down,

Jamie could see the array of abandoned utilitarian icons in great contrast to their feet clothed in uncomfortable but gratifyingly opulent knock-off Gucci Core boots.

They could not simply lose a number or block a contact to be free of this problem. This one was to last forever. The idea had previously terrified Jamie but now, in this cold and dark area of bare concrete and graffiti walls, they were just angry. Really angry. The kind of anger where everyone was to blame except one person.

Feeling the anger well up inside them, Jamie took their hands from the pocket of the over-sized hoodie enveloping them and began to clench. Over and over again. Anything to try and vent this new intensity. A steel pipe, just under a metre long, lay by the side of the road.

No more going out. No future.

Jamie reached down and picked up the pipe. The cold feel and satisfying weight felt right in their manicured hands.

I'll never get a job in a salon now. I'll never make anything iconic if I'm pushing a button in some factory.

Further up the road, Jamie passed a rubbish bin. Bolted to the ground, its stocky metal body stood in peaceful defiance of their mood. Anger boiled and burnt inside their tiny body. Mixing with wine, it called for a reaction. This internal peace could not last. This centre could not hold.

This isn't fair. I didn't do anything wrong.

The sound was loud and produced a great echo. The reverberations travelled up the pipe to Jamie's slender arms. The part of the bin which Jamie had hit showed paint damage but not a dent. It did not share their pain and this was unacceptable.

More and more echoes and more and more reverberations as Jamie struck the lonely rubbish bin over and over again. Eventually there was no winding up for a clean strike. Jamie was simply letting it all out. Every party they would not be able to attend. Every person they would not be able to charm. Every opportunity they could not consider. The accumulated collapse of all these hypothetical futures turned to fuel in Jamie's arms.

The bin, once daring and solid as reality itself, was now bent and broken. Jamie knew the noises would bother local tenants but they didn't care. Right now, Jamie wanted everyone to hear their strength. In fact, they wanted everyone to share their feelings and fear them.

Looking to finish the job, Jamie threw the pipe down and moved to the side. Kicking and pushing, Jamie could feel the bin come untethered from its previous position of contentment. The damage being applied to Jamie's now, not so opulent Gucci boots, was of no concern to them. Neither was the dirt on their hands of the bruises they had accumulated.

Eventually, as all things do, the bin fell. Coming undone after one of Jamie's kicks, it fell to the floor. It did not ask for help, cry or even ask stupid questions. Instead, it just lay there, bent, defeated and completely beyond help.

Turning away without a second look at the pathetic sight, Jamie knew this was not their usual behaviour. They had always considered themselves evolved beyond the animalistic catharsis of violence, but as they continued to walk home to endure what would undoubtedly be a long night of worrying (the first of a lifetime), Jamie felt right. The bin had been bolted to the ground. Its metal roots had run deep into the concrete flesh of Jamie's world and right now, the world really deserved a good beating.

Chapter 5

Wherein we
breathe and
become
pleasantly
anonymous.

(5)

Was it an azure or maybe more of a cerulean? Orion couldn't really decide on the shade of blue sky, which was especially annoying as he was viewing this particular evening scenery from the imaginary window in Dr Fallon's office. Unbeknownst to him, what lay just beyond that wall was not one colour but many. The end of another day had produced the full, beautiful spectrum that accompanied a sunset. That was always Orion's problem. Too much blue on the mind. Not nearly enough pink.

"So how did this episode compare to the initial one months ago?" That's what Dr Fallon had asked. Now, Orion, head still filled with shades of sky, was asked to relive not only one attack but also the most recent.

"It was nowhere near as bad as the first one, thankfully, but it was different. I could almost see my thought process this time. I knew what was happening before it all went down. I suppose it's like making love. All the element of surprise was gone and as soon as I knew what was happening, I just waited until it was over,"

"I mean, I think we both know that comparison is a Freudian's field day," quipped Dr Fallon.

"Ya, I knew it as soon as I said it. You have

permission to make notes in your pad without judgment from me."

Dr Fallon didn't need to be told twice. She swiped the small tablet on her lap and finished making a small entry before looking back to Orion. "So, this is when you found the poster on the notice board?"

"It was right next to a notice for a Queer Youth Summer Camp and one for yet another bake sale."

"And you felt that parading in front of a crowd in fetish gear was a more mentally healthy choice than working with youths or throwing back a muffin or two?"

"Why, doctor, I think that life should accommodate many contradictory facets."

"I see, and did you want that on a T-shirt or tattooed on the small of your back?"

Orion threw his best blank face at this desperately unfunny mental health professional. "You know, you're quite cheeky for a therapist."

"I know, my wife tells me that same thing. Moving on, though, I'd like to talk about this contest and why you think it appeals to you as a creative outlet."

He had been asking himself much the same question for over two weeks now. He would be lying if he said there was no sexual aspect whatsoever to the prospect but mainly, he adored the aesthetic. Perhaps, it was exactly what he had been searching for all this time. Somewhere he wouldn't be stereotyped and where he could merge the best parts of who he was and who he wanted to be.

"I just think it would be fun. I mean, I like the

materials and the looks and, I dunno. I mean, I know not everyone needs therapy but I'm also sure that everyone is a little afraid of being seen and being the centre of scrutiny but when I think of being on that stage and seeing what I can do and what I can contribute and literally wearing the history and legacy that comes with the scene, I dunno. I just don't think that I'll be that scared. Also, I think part of it is definitely like a test. Like if I can get on stage and show my stuff in front of people, that'll probably be a good place."

"Orion, I don't doubt that it would represent a great step forward in your therapy, but do you think a test of that kind is a good idea at the time? I mean, you weren't even on stage at the poetry re—"

"I know," interrupted Orion. "I know what you're going to say and you're right. I wasn't on stage or even speaking to anyone and I had an attack so how could I expect to get on stage in a compromising position in front of people? I know. I really can't explain it to you or probably even to myself. I just have this vision in my head and when I see it, I don't feel scared or anxious. It just feels right."

Dr Fallon took the pad from her lap and placed it on a nearby table before crossing her legs and arms. "You know, it's funny. That's remarkably similar to something a previous patient of mine once said. For some reason, more than anything, they wanted to be a drag king. We spoke about if for a while and even though I felt it was not the best move for them, they're were determined. Eventually, the big day came of their first performance and I remember them telling me that for the first time in their life, they felt like everyone in the room was on their side. They invited me to one of their shows. I couldn't go, of course, but I did see her perform a few years later, long after she had finished her therapy, and I have to say, I'm not sure what did more good – my sessions or her art. It was really something to see."

Orion had never thought about comparing fetish events to drag before but supposed that most of the key elements were the same.

The vision and the preparation.

The changing and the altering.

Then, finally, the presentation and the prestige.

A modern metamorphosis.

Smiling with moist eyes, Orion wanted to thank Dr Fallon for the rare incident of her sharing. "I think that everyone in this room is already on my side."

She could only laugh and return his smile. "With that in mind, I guess when you get on stage, it won't feel like the first time but it will still feel good."

And feeling good was half the battle.

*****

"I got into the scene in my teens and then just kept going. You know, attending some conventions and looking to see what was available online and locally. There was some good stuff but I still went out to vanilla places wearing a chain with a padlock or something and so many people would comment and after I explained, they would tell me they'd love to get into gear but didn't know where to start."

The bulging bicep bear was speaking to Orion next to small table of teas and coffees in the main room of a local event hall. GearMaster2020 (Benny to his friends) spoke with slight lisp and gestured emphatically with his large muscular hands. At the risk of sounding overly graphic, Orion thought he was pretty nifty looking.

"So, a few of us made a plan and formed the local Kink Society and we contacted larger organisations and got accreditation for our titles and now some of our winners can travel the world and compete with the best. I was actually up for Mr International Leather before."

"Oh, wow, that's a global title?" asked Orion.

"Yup. I went national four years ago and won so I flew the flag abroad. I really went for it. I was working out constantly 'cause I had this idea of a beastly, muscly aesthetic."

Orion could only glance fleetingly at the more exposed parts of Benny's torso (Benny had worn a sleeveless T-shirt to this particular event) and though his curves and angles did look naturally grown, there was nothing unbeastly about them, save for them also being a beauty.

This was fun. Orion had arrived over half an hour ago, less nervous than expected but still wary of the unknown. To his surprise, dressed in appropriately casual leather boots and vest, he had been able to meander and talk his way to this point with admirable confidence. First, he spoke to a fellow contestants Gaz and Astra about how it was their respective first times and what tawdry gear they had amassed as hopeful amateurs, and now with Benny, one of the organisers of the event. Several more had shown up until twenty or so people stood around, chatting and waiting for the organisers to make opening announcements.

"Do I need to think of a scene name?" asked Orion.

"Nah, not really. Some people like to and all the pups do but that's just for fun and pups love to have fun."

"Will there be pups be competing at this event?"

"Always! There will definitely be a bunch there as well as other people. Every contest we have is a really cool showcase for people. You would be absolutely gagged at some of the stuff people come up with. I swear, sometimes I'm just looking at the crowd, completely in awe of some of the looks people put together. It's cool because when you see people at your event walk around, or even crawl sometimes, in latex and chains and collars and they just seem so completely happy and at ease and it reminds me why I helped set up this club."

As intimidating as it was hearing about people's creations and looks, Orion couldn't help but feel exited. After all, he was not without creativity himself. Not content to simply strut around in a head-to-toe leather uniform, he was already conceiving of ways to stand out from the rest of the competition.

Speaking of competition, just as Orion was preparing to ask Benny another question, a tall person in pale makeup, with long green hair and the most exquisite pair of thigh-high rubber boots walked to the head of the room and called for attention. They had it before they even spoke.

"Hello, my beauties. God, what a gorgeous bunch of contestants we have this year. The crowd will absolutely love you all and I can already tell that the judges will have a tough time deciding. For the newbies here, I'm that veritable demon of desire, Goddess Kira, they/them pronouns. I'm one of the organisers of the Alt-Kink Society along with Benny, Raven and Trick the Heartbreaker. When we first started this contest three years ago, we had only four contestants. Today, there are fifteen people here looking to win the Alt-Kink Society title for 2021."

A round of applause rightly followed this enthusiastic reading of statistics.

"So, in a few minutes, I'm going to explain the contest and the rules and why we have this little meeting a few months before the contest is actually due but first, before any of you sad and desperate souls fall in love with me, I'm going to have last year's winner and current title holder say a few words. Please welcome someone who has been a great ambassador for our community, Matthew!"

Matthew? Benny must be right, not everyone needed a scene name.

Another round of applause began for the short but exuberantly youthful figure standing close to Goddess Kira. They wore leather jeans and a branded Alt-Kink

Society T-shirt all topped off with a red and black sash across their torso. Their smile and reaction to the applause gave Orion the impression of someone who wasn't used to attention but carried it well.

"Thanks very much, Goddess. I'm Matthew, he/him pronouns. I was only given this sash six months ago, but I can say that I've loved every minute of it and I plan to go on loving it right up until one of you handsome devils prises it from my old, withered hands. It's such a great thing to be given validation over your interests. We all know that very often we're painted as freaks or dangerous people who only like kink gear for depraved reasons and while there's nothing wrong with that, growing up I always thought that there was something more. I can't speak for all of you, but I always say that the reason I joined the scene and competed for this title was not to change myself but to expand myself. To take on a different viewpoint and know that it was okay to feel confident in the aesthetic that attracted me. Smaller titles like this one offer us that opportunity and I hope that as you go through the contest, you'll work hard not to win or outshine anyone else, but to push yourself, expand yourself and contribute to the community that will accept you for who you are. I know I'm rambling now so I'll just say that I look forward to getting to know all of you over the next few months and I hope that you join in our efforts to strip away the shame and taboo unfairly attributed to the kink scene, forever."

Applause and hoots rang from the crowd. Orion leaned over to burly Benny. "Wow, that was something."

"Ya, he's great at that. Last year he wasn't the strongest on his aesthetic, but he totally won us over on the talent and interview section. We had to give him the sash. He's done a great job so far; just look around."

Interview section. Orion had not thought of that. He was confident in the looks he had in mind and had a stringent workout routine planned for the next few months but the prospect of providing eloquent answers in front of a crowd worried him.

What kind of world is this where you can't even skate by on your physical appearance?

Orion could only think as to what might happen. Slowly, the self-replicating nature of anxiety began to trickle into motion. Thinking about experiencing anxiety was leading to increased anxiety levels and so on and so on until Orion was sure he'd have to make an abrupt and unavoidably obvious exit from the room. Would this be the end of his foray into self-realisation?

No, Orion thought to himself. *Everything is fine. We don't have to speak in front of everyone today. Plus, everyone is looking so obviously at Goddess Kira that it would be the act of an extreme narcissist to presume that they were all secretly thinking about you. We're safe.*

That's it.

In and out.

Orion steadied his breath and continued to look forward as the creeping feeling in the base of his skull dissipated and his heart returned to its regular pace. He felt safe or at least, pleasantly anonymous. Also, and Orion wasn't sure how he felt admitting this to himself, the presence of other contestants who were people of colour, were a source of comfort to him. Earlier, while walking there, he had hoped that he would not be the first. It was a consistently admirable but tedious experience.

Goddess Kira hugged the gregarious Matthew and then returned to the head of the room.

"A tough act to follow. I guess that's why he won last year. So, I'm sure some of our contestants, as well as some of our more forgetful returners, are wondering about the rules of this contest. I'm sure you'll be absolutely tickled when I tell you that it's pretty simple. The event will be on five months from now so that's just one night. We've broken it down into three sections: Gear, Interview and Talent. Gear is obviously where you'll be allowed to show off your looks. Anything will be accepted as long as it has a kink aesthetic so please get creative. Interview will be a question or series of questions for each contestant about what the scene means to them and how it's affected their lives. Finally, talent. All talents will be accepted. The stranger and more obscure the better. In the first year of this contest, one of our contestants literally went on stage and finger painted. It was iconic and so funny."

Talent show? Finger painting? Funny?

Orion could feel the familiar tightening in his chest. He had assumed that in a debased and perverse contest like this, his look would simply serve as his talent. Now, to his dismay, this gothic siren was telling him that he had to deliver substance on stage. Reaching beyond the banality of a well-polished boot or new Regulation rubber, he would actually have to insist his unique personality upon the crowd and judges.

Orion looked around the room to see if any of his fellow contestants were experiencing trepidation at this news. To his eyes, they all seemed tranquil. His innocent mind continued to race and worry, blissfully unaware of the motivations and thoughts of the room's other occupants. One of them was in the grips of alcohol withdrawal and had to concentrate on keeping their hands from shaking. One of them was new to the city and thought this would be an interesting way to make friends. One of them would experience the death of a loved one in four months and would have to drop out of the contest. One was on their break from work, one was listening to all of this in a second language and one was simply having a good day. The ever-present internal minutiae of other people was lost on Orion. Not selfishly but perhaps, out of necessity.

And also, a small bit selfishly.

"We have no elimination rounds or anything stupid like that," said Goddess Kira. "Every single one of you will have the chance to show your stuff and stay with the contest right until the very end. As soon as everyone is done, the four judges will deliberate and choose a winner. Now, as you've probably guessed, the reason we have this little get-together so far before the contest is that we know looks and talents can take time, so we like to give people plenty of notice. I'm sure your brilliantly dirty minds are already buzzing with ideas and you probably definitely need time to prepare. Just like Matthew said, this isn't about beating other people, it's about pushing yourself and making something of which you can be proud. If you're looking for drama and backstabbing, take that stuff to the bigger contests. One thing we like to do here is make sure we all know who we're helping push themselves and we like to do that by just going around, identifying who we are in whatever degree makes us comfortable and maybe speak a small bit about why we're in this contest. Is there anyone who'd like to go first?"

Several people raised their hands. Orion was not among them. Goddess Kira pointed to a tall blond man across the room.

"Um, hi, everyone. I'm Aleksander, he/him pronouns. Before I say anything, I just want to say how excited I am for this contest. I've spoken to a few of you so far and I'm really looking forward to seeing you bring your best. You can be sure that I'll do the same. When I was younger and living in Szczecin in Poland, I used to go to Berlin on the weekends with my friends. I really liked the city and all the strange looks and the more I started hanging out in East Berlin when I got a little older, the more I met my queer family and the more I got into the scene. Obviously, the leather scene has always been big in Berlin so I just found so much history and tradition and I absolutely loved it. I was so fascinated by the reclamation of the kind of uber-masculine imagery like leather and uniforms and how they could be used for creative purposes. Trailblazers like Peter Berlin really inspired me and kept my interest all these years so when I moved here ten months ago, finding out if there was a scene was the top of my priorities. Seriously, I knew where to find a good bootblack here before I even found my local shop. When I heard about this contest, I thought it would be fun. I've been in some similar ones back home so I think I know what to expect but I would definitely love to be surprised by one of you. So, ya, I suppose that's me. Thanks."

Aleksander was the first to speak among the crowd. The room rewarded him with a genuine round of applause. When it was over, a figure of adorable mischief was given her chance to speak.

"Hi, everyone, I'm Chandra, she/her pronouns. No, your eyes are not failing you, I am a girl." Most of the room took Chandra's cue and allowed themselves to laugh. "I've been with the pup scene here in town for years now and when I started, I was definitely the first girl and was definitely the first straight girl. As you can imagine, things were a bit funny in the beginning. Some of the more fascistic kinksters didn't know how to handle me. Still, I had tons of support and I'm happy to say that I find things much better now. I am no longer the only girl on the scene although I do feel very privileged to be so engrossed in a scene traditionally occupied solely by proud and creative queer people. As to why I'm in this contest, well, I'm looking to expand some of my looks and I also think it's important to fly the pup flag in any contest I can." A singular hoot of approval came from among the crowd. "Thank you, yes, so that's me. I really look forward to this contest and behold me, I am Chandra, Moon Queen of all Pups!"

Another round of applause for Pup Chandra who more than won over the crowd with her brazenness. Next, was a dark-haired figure who, up to now, had been leaning against a wall toward the back of the room. Orion could not help but make note of his confident aura and handsome features. He was instantly enamoured.

"Hey, guys. I'm Zhang Wei, he/him pronouns. Just listening to those stories and talking to some people here, it's clear that I'm probably the newest to the scene. I've kind of only been active for around seven months now. I'm absolutely loving it, by the way. I first got introduced to the kink scene and the events and meet ups by my boyfriend. Um, it's actually a 'how did you meet' story and no one likes those so I'll keep it brief. I was out once and I first met my boyfriend Markus. I don't want to get sappy but I fell hard when I saw him. He was wearing all the things I had always wanted to wear out. He had the biggest pair of boots laced up right to his knees as well as a leather harness, a collar, a sleeveless latex shirt and the coolest retro punk hairstyle and makeup. It was awesome to see. Anyway, we started talking and I told him how much I loved his look and everything. Eventually, we get a little closer and Markus gets really nervous. I ask what's wrong and he tells me that he had gotten to that point where he had to tell me that he's trans. When he did that, I was so sad because it was obvious from his tone that some people had reacted badly to that before. Anyway, we start hanging out more and eventually Markus tells me some bad stuff from his past and how some people did react badly because they felt they'd been lied to or whatever. When I asked him how he handled all that, he told me that being in the scene, being able to dress how he wanted and being able to express himself in a way which made him feel so in control of his own identity was a huge help. After that, I stopped caring what people thought, changed my aesthetic to what I wanted and started showing up to events and meet ups with beautiful people like you."

The crowd gave off a third round of applause, louder than both the previous ones. Orion, feeling the need to wipe the tears from his eyes, blamed his medication before remembering that he was allowed to cry at an emotional story if he was so inclined.

"So, there you have it, people who are trans and life-affirming fetish gear. To quote my uncle, this is the future we Liberals want."

"It can't come soon enough," shouted Goddess Kira before gesturing to a rugged gentleman among the crowd. Sporting a strong chin of stubble and temples of short, slightly greying hair, he shifted uneasily.

"Wow," he said, "that is quite an act to follow. I feel slightly out of place because I have no great story of discovery or hardship. I guess I can just say that I love the gear scene because I always have. I got into it in my late teens and I rocked some serious looks throughout my twenties. Back then, things were pretty basic. The whole Tom of Finland look was still big, and the term castro clone was thrown at me on more than one occasion, and I loved it. I don't want to drone on so I'll just say that contests like this help keep me young and I hope to bring some old-school magic to the table."

So, on it went. Many more contestants came forward and took the opportunity to speak about themselves. A very natural human instinct. Orion was not one of them. He had never been to a group therapy meeting or counselling session, but he imagined it would be something similar. After a while, he did feel like he knew the other people in the room more than he had any right to. It was oddly soothing. The veil of unknowing instantly attached to strangers had been lifted and Orion found it difficult to imagine that these people were secretly talking about him. Instead, he thought about their desires and what they hoped to achieve in this contest.

Hours later, as Orion lay in bed, he would regret not stepping forward to add his own story to the group knowledge. He wondered how honest he would have chosen to be and whether the crowd would have applauded his bravery.

Brave. Is that what we are? he thought.

More and more thoughts, not all of them pleasant, raced through Orion's mind as he tried to attain the peace of sleep. This was always a prime time for his brain to torture him but, as he lay down, staring into the quiet darkness, his final thoughts were not of self-pity or worry but rather of the comfort he felt today and how he had navigated the social setting with apparent ease. He wasn't sure if it was a great cause for celebration. He only knew that it was progress.

Chapter 6

Wherein you can't even spew uninformed, hate-filled bile without the PC police jumping down your throat.

(6)

"Make sure they don't try to convert you."

That was Akib's last piece of advice to Jamie. A humorous but nonetheless sound warning. The repetition of domestic comforts did have their seductive charm and even Jamie wasn't naive enough to deny that.

Humorous or not, Jamie could use all the advice they could take for tonight's adventure. Walking down the quiet row of identical homes, they were preparing to meet Caoimhe's parents for evening dinner. They had previously been introduced to Joe and Emma on two different occasions but these meetings had never extended to the preparation and consumption of food. From what Caoimhe had told them, her parents wanted to get to know Jamie better, size them up and decide as to whether they would make an appropriate father. The thought of it made Jamie uncomfortable. This was not the type of scrutiny to which they were used.

Adding to their discomfort, Jamie couldn't stop rearranging their clothes. Dressed from head to toe in the most unnatural style, Jamie was sporting scared, conservative chic. The tan khaki trousers and pale blue, long sleeve shirt made Jamie feel invisible in the most treacherous way possible. A stinging betrayal of a lifetime of brave fashion choices. Even Jamie's hair, which usually boasted a bright colour chosen on a whim, was now combed and styled to neat, plain brunette perfection.

Not even the three shots Jamie had taken earlier could relieve the tension in their shoulders. Instead, they simply walked toward the front door, drew a deep breath and pressed the bone-chillingly whimsical doorbell.

Caoimhe answered, gave Jamie a big smile and greeted them with a hug. Even now, Jamie could not help but admit that she really was something. They had not seen her mood drop once throughout this entire ordeal.

"Aw, you look so adorable," she said, taking a second to glance Jamie up and down. "Did you dress down for dinner?"

"It seemed like right move to make," they answered. "If I want to get the blessing from Ron and Nancy in there."

"Oh, stop. This isn't about approval. Joe and Emma are very much aware that this baby is coming whether they approve of you or not. Tonight is just about getting to know you. They're excited. Truth be told, I am too. I had a feeling that you wouldn't know how to act but I never expected this kind of look. Are you applying for a home loan?"

"I'm glad you're enjoying yourself. I feel so uncomfortable, I feel like I could climb up these walls like some drunk, queer insect."

"Oh, boo hoo, poor Jamie has to put on a shirt with sleeves and a mid-section for a change. You won't get any sympathy from the pregnant lady about you being uncomfortable," she said while straightening the buttons on Jamie's shirt-shaped prison. "Oh, and my big bro, Nathan, is coming to dinner as well. He'll be here soon."

Oh great, thought Jamie. *Just what we need. An unstable element. With my luck, he'll probably be gorgeous and generous. A perfect distraction.*

The large and pink-faced figure of Caoimhe's father, Joe, came from around the corner. Stretching out his arm for a handshake, he was dressed alarmingly similar to Jamie, save for a salmon pink shirt in place of Jamie's blue. Later in the night, Jamie would wonder if a salmon pink shirt was a mandatory component in the standard, middle-class father's uniform.

"Good to see you, Jim," said Joe while grabbing Jamie's hand. Jamie was not unaccustomed to attention from men of Joe's age but had never really learned to converse with them outside of a more clandestine environment.

"Dad, we've spoken about this. Jamie likes their name the way it is," said Caoimhe.

"No harm meant, it's just easier to remember for me. You don't mind, do you, Jim?"

Before Jamie could say anything or even retrieve their hand from Joe, Caoimhe answered for them. "Jamie does mind. They're just being nice. Now come on, you two, let's go inside."

Jamie was led down a hallway toward the living room. The walls were adorned with pictures – babies, first days at school, graduations, older relatives, uncles no one liked and cousins no one ever really knew. Was it not enough that people had children? Did they need to adorn every inch of their home with documented evidence? Moving slowly down that hallway, with Caoimhe to their front and Joe to their back, Jamie couldn't help but feel they were being led to some sort of gallows. Each and every figure staring down at Jamie was a spectacle to their degradation. Their wide eyes hungry for justice, 'CONFORMITY OR DEATH' they screamed from inside their frames.

As they reached the living room, the slim, apron-clad figure of Emma, Caoimhe's mother, appeared.

"Jamie, so nice of you join us for dinner. Oh, don't you look handsome. Doesn't he look handsome, Joe?"

"Like a little gentleman," Joe answered, sinking into an armchair.

Jamie, not knowing how to respond at first, eventually thought better than to start the night by preaching the proper use of pronouns. Instead, attempting to be as gracious as possible, they produced a dry laugh before catching Caoimhe's eyes. She must have got the signal as her next words were ones of mercy.

"So, who wants a glass of wine?" she asked while unscrewing the metal top from a bottle of white. Jamie was beyond grateful. They could, with a conceded effort that would border on apathy, survive a night of misgendering without the aid of intoxicants but that endeavour would be almost impossible when coupled with their current, relentlessly heterosexual surroundings.

Jamie looked at the room in which they currently sat. It contained a large couch in black leather with two matching armchairs all turned to face an offensively large and centralised flat screen TV. The walls were panelled with wood while the floor, over two shades lighter than the walls, was covered in a PVC faux-wood decking. The corner of the room contained a large wooden display piece holding mismatched pieces from some crystal glass set while the *pièce de résistance* was, by far, the large, framed, by-the-batch print of a sunset that hung over the bare fireplace. Jamie held their glass in such a way as to hide the large gulps they were taking. A necessary step in attempting to numb the draining ache that this house produced.

"So, Jamie. How goes the search for work?" asked Joe.

"Jamie's had some really good prospects recently," Caoimhe answered.

"I'm sure that's true, Caoimhe, but you should probably let him answer for himself. Your mother's always doing that to me, aren't you, Emma?" said Joe while calling into the kitchen.

"What am I doing?" asked a voice from the next room.

"I said you're always speaking for me."

"I can't hear you, Joe. I'm draining the carrots."

Caoimhe's Dad looked back to Jamie and opened his eyes wide in a *see what I mean* fashion. "Women. They'll drive you mad."

Christ! I'm going to need more than wine to get

through this. I wonder, could I hide in the bathroom and message Buy-a-Bag Barry or Share-a-Line Susan to come help? Second thoughts, better not. I have no money or cash to fund that. I gave the last of mine to Luna for sets in her all-female production of Twelve Angry Men at the Queer Resource Centre. I wonder, do they need someone to hair and makeup? Hair and makeup ... Oh, the normies are still waiting for me to answer.

"Work, yes! Ya, Caoimhe is right. I've been visiting salons recently and I know some people on the management team in a few of them and I think I'm really close to getting an apprenticeship."

"Apprenticeship!" exclaimed Joe, looking amused. "I had one of them when I was your age except it was scaffolding in a building site. Never thought it would be the kind of thing you could get in a salon. I suppose the world has changed since I was your age."

If only you knew, Joe.

"Not much money in apprenticeships these days, am I right? Or at least there isn't on the building sites."

Money was everything to these people. Jamie understood that. They valued their security. Their reaffirming comforts. It was enough to make Jamie wish they had prepared a more profitable answer.

"No, not much I suppose but like I said, I do know the management and some of the owners and they said I'd get my share of the tips."

Jamie could see that Joe was unimpressed. How in the world could Jamie not want to jump onto the first vaguely well-paying job possible and endeavour to live in a tacky, wood-panelled baby factory? Quick, how could Jamie turn their knowledge of throwing looks together and low-end fashion shoots into a positive?

"I'm also looking into other careers. Some of my friends work in fashion and I'd love to get involved in the production or marketing side of the industry."

"Oh, how did you learn about that kind of stuff?" asked Joe.

Don't say drag.

Don't say drag.

Don't say drag.

"It's just stuff I picked up from my mother," answered Jamie.

Caoimhe reached over and gave her unspoken approval by gently squeezing Jamie's forearm. They responded by taking another sip of wine. The dry, tangy gulp was a welcome but far too short break from conversation. Then, relief came in the form of a homemade meal.

"Dinner's ready!" yelled Emma from the next room.

Caoimhe, Joe and Jamie went to meet Emma at the dining table where five plates of well-presented food were waiting. To their recollection, the last time Jamie had eaten was a late breakfast the previous day. While they certainly didn't feel like eating anything, they knew it would be extremely rude to refuse. Jamie took another large sip of wine and wondered where their body found its daily energy.

Caoimhe stared at the plates in front of her. "Mom, I told you that Jamie was a vegan."

Jamie looked down to see that while four of the plates contained a portion of steak, one of them, presumably set for them, boasted a serving of fish.

"I know you did," said Emma. "I know all the young people aren't eating meat and dairy and gluten and plastic straws and everything these days. It's the new trend. I just thought that since we're all eating dinner together, Jamie might like some fish. It's not meat so it should be okay. Plus, Jamie, you're only skin and bones. It'll be good for you."

Jamie wasn't quite sure what about that sentence to hate the most and in what order. The complete disregard for new ideas, the condescending infanticisation or the odd and completely - uncalled for reference to their weight. It was awful. Almost as awful as the prospect of swallowing down this hunk of fish.

"Mom, vegans don't eat fish or anything that …"

"No, Caoimhe, it's fine," interrupted Jamie. "It won't kill me, after all. Plus, it looks lovely."

Just as soon as all four of them had sat down to the table, there came a noise from the kitchen of a door closing and someone entering the house.

"Hello?" called a voice.

"Oh, that will be Nathan, Caoimhe's brother. We're in here," called Emma.

Into the living room stepped Nathan, a tall and typical figure in his late twenties. He kissed his mother on the cheek before acknowledging that Jamie was joining them for dinner. "So, this must be the new father," he said, extending his arm for a handshake.

"I suppose that's me. I'm Jamie, Nathan. It's nice to meet you."

"Ya, I bet it is. Well, it's cool to meet the guy who's making me an uncle. I gotta say, I'm a little surprised. You're not Caoimhe's usual type."

Jamie wasn't sure how to take that, even if it was definitely true. "Ya, I got that impression when we first met."

Nathan, who was now in his seat, began cutting into his steak. The rest of the family followed his lead. Jamie picked up their fork and knife and decided to start slowly with some of the vegetables.

"So, what are we talking about? What did I miss?" asked Nathan.

"Jamie was just telling us about looking for a job," said Joe. "What was it, Jamie, something in textiles?"

"Ya, textiles," said Jamie, lying out of politeness. "Textiles or fashion. My friend Akib sometimes works on designing outfits and they were saying they could introduce me to some local seamstresses."

"What do you mean by <u>they</u>?" asked Nathan, forking a wad of beef into his mouth. "Is Akib one friend or are they conjoined at the hip?"

Emma didn't react but Joe couldn't help but let out a laugh at his terribly funny son's terribly clever joke.

Jamie held their mouth slightly agape while they looked toward Caoimhe. She gave back a sympathetic look that seemed to say *I know, it's okay. I know.*

Ah, thought Jamie. *So, Nathan is this guy.* This was nothing unique or new to Jamie. They had sat through it before. The jokes, the comments and the casual dismissal of their very existence. As much as Jamie hated this guy, this was not the time for confrontation. This was a bank robbery. A rare caper into their world. In, get the approval from Caoimhe's family and get out. After all, it wasn't a lie of omission if their values force you into silence.

"No," said Jamie. "Akib prefers gender neutral, they/them pronouns. We've been best friends for ten years."

"Pronouns, yes, of course. That's the big word of the year. I hear they have around ten or twenty pronouns for someone now and we're all supposed to learn them or the PC police will be after us. I mean, no offence, 'cause I obviously don't know much about it, but when I was in school, saying they or them meant there was more than one person. Is that what it's like? These people feel like schizophrenics or something?"

"I think it's more like they feel neither male nor female so neither he or she is appropriate," said Caoimhe, attempting to bridge the gap. She was sweet for trying but Nathan, being that guy, just wouldn't drop the issue. It was impossible for him to read the room and realise that Jamie would rather be talking about anything else. This was the thick and salty senselessness built up from the slow, sedentary life without persecution or seclusion.

"Ya, ya, I get that part of it but I still don't know what that means. I mean, how you feel inside doesn't affect who you are. A black guy who feels white doesn't just turn white. Hell, I feel like a millionaire on the inside. Hey, government, where are my millions?"

This time both Joe and Emma shared a giggle. Caoimhe took a sip of wine (her first of the night). Jamie could see that she was embarrassed.

"I don't care who likes to wear a dress or likes to dress up but it's really just science and as far as I'm concerned, if you're born with girl parts, you're a girl and if you're born with boy parts, you're a boy."

"Nathan! Will you just drop it" said Caoimhe, abandoning her gentle approach. Nathan looked to his mum and dad for support. The look on his face was one of someone who was rarely challenged on their opinions.

"Alright, jeez, I'm sorry. I was just thinking. I know that's not allowed in today's climate, but I thought it would be okay in my own home. You know, have a little free speech with my steak. Plus, Jamie looks like he's been around a few times. What do you think, Jim?"

I think you're a tasteless, senseless, crude, ass with no sense of empathy and undoubtedly has a social circle of people who are basically just copies of you. I think you're small, I think you're boring and more than anything, I think I'd be happy if that steak became lodged in your festering, putrid throat. Just for a minute or two.

That's what Jamie wanted to say and as far as they were concerned, Nathan would be getting the kind version. If Akib was here, they would have torn this troglodyte's head off.

"I don't really have an opinion on it but like I said,

Akib is my friend." Jamie hoped that this response might be subtle enough to remain non-confrontational but definitive enough to change the conversation. Of course, Jamie knew that was wishful thinking. They knew the score as well as any queer person just trying to live their lives. This was a forever conversation. It and others just like it had existed through time. Its content, rhythm and cadence would reverberate back to the great, queer, pre-dark age cultures of the ancient past and forward to the gender non-conforming, mega societies of the future. Always, there would be someone like Nathan. Someone who was not just stupid, an excusable sin of any life form, but also loud, smug and repetitive in the most corrosive way possible.

"There, sis, see. Jim doesn't mind. Like he said, we all have friends who are different to us. Not a big deal. Plus, you two should be thinking more and more about this stuff since you're bringing a little nipper in to the world. That's the next stage now. He'll probably come out and the doctor won't even let you call him a boy or give it a boy's name until he's old enough to decide his own gender, whatever that means. I see that kind of stuff all the time on the news and during those Pride marches they have. Children with dyed hair and rainbow everything."

"Now I do think that is quite enough, you know. Bringing children into everything. Kids should just be allowed to be kids," said Emma.

"Oh, careful, Mum. You can't say that kind of stuff. It's damaging to their culture. That's actually another thing that I don't understand. All the campaigns for marriage and stuff and they always say that they're regular people and just wanted to be treated fairly because they're the same but then they turn around and say that they have a separate culture. Like, so which one is it? Are they different or are they the same? I mean, if they were all from a different country or something, that would make sense but how do you make a culture around guys liking other guys or people changing their sex? Do you see what I'm saying, Jim?"

Jamie did know what Nathan was saying. They had known it all their life. The unoriginal, squawking prejudice of tiny people like Nathan was an all too familiar aperitif to this family meal and meals just like it all across the world. In darker moments, when things had been shouted from moving cars, Jamie wondered about the dangerous, life-giving fire in the hearts of people like Nathan and his equally ignorant cohorts.

Was Jamie such a threat to them? They didn't think so.

Looking to shake off these thoughts, Jamie reached over to hold Caoimhe's hand. She seemed surprised and happy that Jamie was keeping their cool. She smiled that perfect smile and Jamie felt better. Nathan became a drone in the background. Looking at her, Jamie told themselves that they cared for her and for the baby.

They smiled back and squeezed just a little tighter. *Everything is fine,* Jamie thought to themselves but secretly, in their heart, they looked at Caoimhe and wondered about that fire and the sad, empty embers it might leave in its wake.

*****

Quake was uncharacteristically dark and quiet. The tantalising vibration had been reduced to a tense atmosphere. Exactly three minutes after this rare quiet had overtaken the ground floor, a bar of light emerged as two figures walked through the front entrance. As they did, the lights were turned back on quickly and the vibration returned, strong as ever.

"SURPRISE!" yelled the club's many patrons.

Gabe, who was a local writer known to many and who had recently announced themselves as a trans-man, was the intended target of this surprise party. Along with lights, a floor full of friends and acquaintances, Gabe was greeted by a large banner tied above the main dance floor. Printed in blue, four foot letters were the words, **'IT'S A BOY!'**.

"I love the sign," commented one of Quake's patrons.

"You should. One less sign to be used in those creepy gender-reveal parties for babies," responded another.

Gabe was beyond the point of joyful tears. Reaching out and hugging everyone he encountered, he was just another person on the wild and often dangerous journey of self-discovery. Tomorrow and each subsequent day would bring new challenges but at that moment, bathed in the recognition and affection of his local queer community, he could not help but feel proud, loved and finally, miraculously, himself.

An hour or so passed and Jamie, who was one of the organisers of this event, sat with familiar company.

"He just kept droning on and on. He wouldn't shut up and the more he spoke, the less he ate and so the longer I just had to sit and listen. It was awful. Eventually I just choked down the fish I was given and left. Guys, I'm serious, it was really bad."

After their far too long visit to the other side, Jamie had ran home and changed before heading to Quake for some well-earned decompression.

And drinking.

"I mean, did he apologise or anything?" asked Coach.

"Apologise!" said Shira with a laugh. "Why should he? He was in his house and in his house, he can spew whatever hate he wants. That's what some houses are. Just a bunch of people shouting and agreeing with each other until their opinions bounce from wall to wall like Wi-Fi. This is why group living in nature communes make so much sense. No closed doors."

"Leaving aside that that was by far the most lesbian thing Shira has ever said, I was just asking whether this brother realised you were queer and that you didn't agree with what he was saying?" asked Coach.

Jamie couldn't help but absent-mindedly move ice cubes in their drink with their straw. "It didn't come up."

The silence that proceeded was palpable even

among the bass-heavy Kim Petras remix.

"What do you mean, it didn't come up?" asked Shira. "Was he wearing a blindfold or was he perhaps calling on Skype with no picture or sound?"

"I don't know," answered Jamie. "I don't really know what happened. I mean, I know Caoimhe mentioned something to her family about me but I think when I showed up in my little get up, he must have thought that I was one of the good queers he sees on TV or maybe not queer at all because I got his sister pregnant. That's what really annoys me about all this. It's not that someone is close minded or full of vitriol. You could walk outside and find that anywhere. It's that for some reason, he actually thought I would agree with him. Like we'd bond over our mutual distrust of people we don't understand. The whole thing makes me feel filthy."

Jamie hoped that they were coming off disappointed enough in themselves that no one would be disappointed in them. This seemed to be the case as Shira reached over to palm their shoulder.

"So, did they have like, a big Jesus cross and servants and racist old people?" asked Shira, attempting to lighten the mood.

"They're straight. They're not from the 1920s. It wasn't bad, it was just so much of nothing. Everything was made to stand out as little as possible."

Looking to shake the memory, Jamie took a deep draught from the straw in front of them and breathed in the familiar air of the place they loved. "I feel better now, though. Much better. These lights seem to be refuelling me. Giving me strength."

"That's queer photosynthesis," said Akib.

"Is that even a real thing?" asked Coach.

"Oh, it absolutely is, especially for a delicate rose like Jamie, here. It happens when a queer person has spent too long on the other side. Then suddenly you come back to a queer space where you feel safe and you know you'll receive basic human respect, and you find that it actually gives you energy. Like, you can literally feed off the atmosphere."

"Can we ferment this nourishing atmosphere?" asked Coach, "because if not, I'm going to need help carrying my round of drinks back."

Coach, Shira and Akib headed away to the bar leaving Jamie to sit with Ren near the dance floor. The occupants seemed distant to Jamie. It seemed to them that they were sitting next to huge body of water, peering at unattainable sea life. Ren stared out with a cool fascination as if they might spring into action at any second. Jamie wondered what calm and fearless thought processes were behind those green eyes. Could they dive hand in hand with Ren into that body of water where responsibility dissolved away? Up to now, that had always been an option.

"I don't know what I'm going to do," said Jamie with a sigh.

A few second of silence followed. "Of course you do," said Ren. "You've always known. You've known it since you were a teenager trying on clothes they told you were only for women. You knew it when you were a child and you couldn't relate to what people wanted from you. You even knew it before you were born. Even then, thousands of years of queer experience lived in you. It ran through every cell in your body just like it does now. Centuries of experience boiled and condensed to make you. They live in you now. I find that if you stop and listen, you can almost hear them and their stories. The love, the persecution, the pain and the joy. That's our connection. That is our birth right. We do honour to their lives and their legacy by living exactly how we want. I know you feel it, even if you don't. I first felt it in a dream. I was having my top surgery and I went under. I was nervous but afterward, I wasn't nervous anymore and I wasn't nervous because I finally knew the truth. Every time someone chooses to be who they are, the universe becomes a more interesting and worthwhile place. I know it can be easy to forget that sometimes and I know you have problems, but I also know that all of what you're experiencing is from you feeling alone or unloved. All of which is untrue, Jamie. You are not alone. You can never be alone, and you are loved so very much. We won't discard your worries to an uncaring world. We will always be with you. Myself and the billions who came before you. Look across that dance floor. What you're seeing is not just some people dancing. What you see are beings crying out for a connection and they're crying out because that is the root of what we do. It's not selfish or inconvenient. We are trying to build a connection. A true and honest connection. I'm going to stand up now and walk onto that dance floor. I'm going to connect with someone, and I hope that when I do, it will be with a real person living in the most honest way they can. When you're ready, you should come and join me."

With that, Ren stood up and walked slowly onto the dance floor. Jamie could have sworn that a mist seemed to surround them. Its neon shapes moved and swirled around Ren until they could be seen no more.

They were with the sea life now.

"Coach and Shira are still at the bar arguing about something. I managed to grab you a beer," said Akib on their return.

Jamie accepted the cold bottle into their hand before setting it down. "Akib, when you went for your top surgery and you went under, did you dream?"

"Definitely, I had these two very vivid dreams. I remember in the first one I had this dream about the scars I knew that I would have after the surgery on my chest and just along my ribs. I was kind of nervous about them but somehow, in the dream, I started to think of them like the scars of Christ after their ribs were pierced with a spear and after that I knew that I would love my scars for as long as I had them."

"And the other dream?"

Akib smiled as though the question itself made them happy. "My second dream was the only dream that's really worth having. I dreamed of a better world."

Chapter 7

Wherein we clap back but ultimately miss the point.

(7)

It's my birth right.
It's my birth right.
It's my birth right.

Jamie had thought about what Ren had said over the past week and now knew what they had to do. They felt almost giddy as they walked down the driveway of Caoimhe's home toward the front door. Caoimhe answered.

"Hi, Jamie." She paused. "You look different."

That was an understatement. Jamie could not be dressed more in contrast to their last visit to Caoimhe's home if they tried. Standing in front of Caoimhe, one hand hanging and one planted blatantly on a dropped hip, was Jamie they/them: a slim, 5'8 figure of incontestable opulence.

Instead of the previous week's brown loafers, Jamie sported a worn but animated pair of 8-eyelet Doc Marten boots with pink laces. Instead of the loose-fitting brown khaki trousers, Jamie wore … very little at all, in fact. That is to say that Jamie's current green, tartan skirt left little to the imagination in the leg department. They had even gone to the trouble of shaving.

Instead of the blue, long sleeve shirt (tucked neatly

into the trousers for that extra effect of anonymity) Jamie wore one of their sleeveless tank tops. This one was white and sported the logo and name for the Canadian band *Lesbians on Ecstasy.*

Instead of their previous plain and pallid visage, Jamie had taken great care on their face. Their eyebrows were tweezed, shaped and then filled, courtesy of a Luxie eyebrow sculpting set borrowed from Akib. Their bronzer and highlight were, in Jamie's never humble opinion, on point. Jamie's mouth shone the full and dark red shine of their arabesque-shade lipstick while a gold-coloured septum ring matched the equally noticeable piercings in either ear.

Finally, Jamie's hair, previously a flat, neat shade of brown, had been shaved on both sides and the remainder dyed. One half sported a shade of light blue and the other, a shade of pink lavender. It would take the initiated less than a second to notice that these colours were chosen to match the shade of Jamie's eye shadow.

"I thought I'd go for a different look this evening. Mmmm, something smells yummy inside."

Caoimhe, with a steely eyed look Jamie had never seen before, kept her position in the doorway. "Jamie, you don't have to do this."

"What? Come in and crack wise with my child's grandparents? Seems pretty natural given the circumstance."

"First of all, I don't like you referring to our child as a circumstance or a situation. Secondly, I know the last visit didn't go so well for you, but you don't need to do this. It's not worth it. If you're looking to pick a fight, this is not the time or place."

Her tone was reasonable and full of sweetness. Any other day, Jamie probably would have been able to hear her. Instead, the excitement from a week of obsession compelled them forward through that front door.

"Caoimhe, I'm just here to see your folks and let them get to know the real me. I promise I'll be good," they lied.

Caoimhe exhaled loudly through her nose before begrudgingly moving aside and allowing Jamie into her home. As they walked down the hallway toward the living room, the static pictures of family occasions looked less intimidating than before. Rather than shouting for conformity, they were forced to bear witness. *SEE ME*, Jamie did scream and the photos did see.

Reaching the end of the runway hallway, Jamie walked into the living room to find Joe, in full salmon pink attire, sitting on one of the black leather armchairs. Jamie could read his expression as they had seen it many times before. The wide eyes. The slightly open mouth. His face was of someone who didn't know whether they should comment on what they were seeing.

"Jamie, welcome back. How are you?" asked Joe, obviously deciding to err on the side of caution. Jamie liked that. Nothing like a little shock and awe to produce some gratifyingly stunned silence.

"I'm doing pretty well, Joseph. I had a fun two weeks. I helped my friends set up this photography showcase with a Mapplethorpe retrospective afterward, then I volunteered at a sexual health and wellbeing seminar at the queer youth resource centre, then I got to a spend a few hours at this queer pet grooming service which was super cute and then finally I went with my friend to a little makeover of theirs and I joined in as you can probably guess. How about you?"

"Oh, we went for a drive ... and then ... we ... umm ... I'm sorry, did you say queer pet grooming service?"

Emma, Caoimhe's mother, walked into the room with apron-clad swiftness. "Dinner will be ready soon." She stopped to closer examine the room's occupants. "Oh, Jamie. You look different."

"Yes, I was just telling Joe here that I had a little makeover. Feels much more like myself."

"Ah. Yes, I see. Caoimhe mentioned that you ... well, that ... anyway, it's good that you're here," she said with an uneasy smile. Jamie could live with unease. In fact, they counted it as a rousing success. The sleek wood panels of this living room had never reflected anything so fabulous in the history of this family. While this was an achievement in itself, Jamie wondered if they could push it further. "So, shall we sit at the table?" they asked.

"Good idea," responded Joe. "Caoimhe, can you get me a drink, please. No wine, I'll take a whiskey."

"Oh, actually that sounds good, Caoimhe. I'd love a whiskey too," said Jamie. Caoimhe complied and threw the contents of a nearby bottle into two short tumblers. Upon receipt, Jamie promptly downed half the glass and noticed that Joe left his on the table, untouched. Jamie could only speculate as to Joe's internal monologue.

Oh no, it drinks whiskey too. It's a man's drink though ... unless ... have I been drinking cross-dressing gay juice this whole time? Sweet salmon coloured mercy! Should I go now and shack up with Hank from the golf club?

Interrupting her husband's worries, Emma placed plates in front of the table's occupants. A breaded, boneless friend looked up at Jamie from their plate.

"Mum, I told you before and last time that Jamie is a vegan."

"Caoimhe, he ate it up last time so I didn't think it would be a big deal."

"Caoimhe, seriously, it's fine," said Jamie, picking up their knife and fork and casually forking a carrot into their mouth. "Plus, this meal looks delicious. I can't wait to eat it. I am going to skip the fish, but these veggies and little potatoes look lovely."

Before Emma could protest, the sound of a door opening came from the kitchen. Taking a sip from his glass, Joe glanced an uneasy look at his wife.

Nathan had arrived.

"Hello, all," said Nathan as he entered the room. "How is every—" he paused to look at Jamie who was slicing up a mini potato. "—one? Jamie, is that you?"

"Who else would it be, you big future uncle? Come and sit down."

Nathan, whose body took on the language of someone who had walked in on a murder scene, looked toward his family.

After a few seconds of noticeable hesitance, Caoimhe spoke.

"Nathan, just sit down. The food is getting cold."

He did so. The table was quiet, save for Jamie's gentle munching.

Getting kind of a creepy hostage situation vibe, thought Jamie. *Better say something.*

"So, Nathan. How is work going?"

"Ya, fine. Are you on your way to a costume party or something?" he asked.

"Nope. I mean, I like to think that life is one big costume party. A ninety or so yearlong celebration," Jamie answered before taking a sip of their drink and returning to their plate as if their answer was the most unremarkable in the world.

"I think," Emma began, "that Nathan was more talking about your outfit. It's definitely different from the last time you were here."

"Oh, right," laughed Jamie, feigning ignorance. "Ya, I suppose it is. I'm non-binary gender-fluid so some days I'll feel like dressing one way and some days I'll feel like dressing a different way. Plus, in the end, it's just clothes so it doesn't matter much but changing your physical appearance can go a long way toward expressing yourself."

Nathan, who had not touched anything on his plate or taken his eyes off Jamie, spoke. "Caoimhe mentioned that you also like boys. Are you trying to tell us that you're a tranny?"

Pausing to mark off *tranny* in their mental bingo sheet of hateful words, Jamie lowered their cutlery, met Nathan's unblinking stare with their own and spoke slowly.

"I'm not trying to tell you that. I'm not trying to tell you anything."

No one moved while the stare down remained unbroken.

Caoimhe, always the peace maker, broke the silence. "Jamie is very expressive with their fashion and stuff. Isn't that right?"

"That's right," said Jamie, breaking eye contact with Nathan and taking one of Caoimhe's free hands in their own. "I have been since I was young. I find it very freeing and very self-actualising."

Their answer had Caoimhe's desired effect. Emma's eyebrows lowered and Nathan even reached for his fork and knife. Perhaps they were content with thinking that Jamie's proclivities were the result of an overly creative personality and, while certainly outside the realm of good taste, were essentially harmless.

Jamie could sense this condescending ease and did not like it.

"And I can't wait to teach it to our child."

The effect was immediate. It was as if Caoimhe's family had suddenly remembered after forgetting that Jamie was the father of her baby. Jamie knew this was the key. In their experience, conventional people disliked the fact that some people were living lives different to theirs, but they lacked the moral high ground from which to criticise. What was not beyond the reach of this close-minded reprimanding was the care of children. They and they alone held supreme authority over the care and upbringing of young humans and all those who wished to participate must fall in line and conform. It was a sting felt by single parents, same sex couples and 'unconventional' families all throughout the world.

"What?" asked Nathan. "You mean you're actually going to teach them about how to dress up and have no gender and stuff?"

"Absolutely," answered Jamie, daring to go further. "Actually, teach might be a bad word. There won't be lessons or anything. I do plan to raise them that way, though. Let them know all about queer culture, the wide spectrum of gender and sexuality expressions and the confining nature of binary thinking. I can't wait."

"So, if it's a boy, you would dress it in a skirt or something for school?"

"I'd let my kid dress however they want as long as it's not revealing or dangerous or something. It'll be good for them. I wish my parents had done the same with me." Jamie thought about asking Nathan if he ever had an urge to put on a skirt when they were young but decided against it.

"And you wouldn't care if they were bullied or anything?"

"If someone was bullying my child, I would hope that the school or other parents would correct their behaviour and not admonish my kid for doing nothing wrong."

"I think Nathan meant more that it might be unfair to paint such a big target on a child's back so early on," said Emma, attempting to clarify her son's prejudice.

"Expressing yourself is not an invitation for abuse and harassment. If there was someone who was bullying people for being who they are, I would suggest that person re-examine their motives."

The not-so-subtle undertone of Jamie's answer was obvious to everyone in the room, even to someone as mentally feeble and narrow as Nathan. In response, he clenched his fist and turned to Caoimhe.

"And you're just okay with that?"

"Nathan, will you please calm down," she asked.

Nathan rose to his feet in response. "No, I will not calm down. This guy comes into our house, essentially cross-dressing, talking about teaching your child about rainbows and third genders and other crap and I'm supposed to just sit and think it's okay? Well, you know what? I don't care what you are or what the hell made you this way. You can't fill a child's head with this kind of nonsense. It will mess them up for life and they'll probably end up even worse than you and you are wrong if you think I'm going to sit here and eat dinner with a freak. Out there you can be what you want but this is my house and I can say what I want."

With all pretence of a polite dinner now gone, Jamie knew their final victory would require calm and resolve.

"This is your house, Nathan, but this is my body and this is mine and Caoimhe's baby. I'm not going anywhere."

A silence filled the room before, without saying a word, Nathan turned on his heels and walked out of the room.

"Nathan, wait!" Emma called as she went after him.

Caoimhe grabbed Jamie by the wrist and pulled them up from their chair. "Can I speak to you outside?" she demanded, albeit in the form of a question.

While being led from the dining room, knowing they would probably never be invited back, Jamie could swear they caught the hint of a smirk on Joe's face.

Hope you enjoyed the show, Joe. I did it for all of us.

Caoimhe dragged Jamie through the kitchen and out the back door until they were standing in the harsh glow of the back garden, motion-activated lamp. Letting go of Jamie's arm, she stood silently with the body language of someone who was waiting for an explanation.

God, she's going to make an excellent mother.

Jamie started. "I think what we can take from this is—."

"You promised! You said you weren't here to pick a fight and you just wanted them to get to know the real you and then the second you're inside, you're just showing off and loving every minute of it. I bet you'll have a great time telling this to everyone later. A great story about how you freaked out the normies and left them speechless. God, what was I thinking?"

Jamie wondered the same thing. What was she thinking? The small circumstance in her womb was half theirs. As it happily and efficiently drained the nutrients from her body, could she not utilise its developing mind in predicting what Jamie was going to do? If not, she was in for a lifetime of surprises as Jamie had no intention of stopping and no intention of apologising for tonight's happy home meal. Quite the contrary, Jamie intended to go on the offensive.

"Hey! I'm sorry if you can't handle who I am or how I live but—"

"HOW DARE YOU!" she yelled. "How dare you for a single second imply that I am not on your side. That I haven't supported you as best I could this entire time. That I haven't defended you, that I haven't been there for you or that I'm somehow grossed out by who you are because that is what you just did with what you did in there and what you just said to me. God, you think the rest of us are just ants crawling around waiting for our chance to sting you and reject you for being who you are so you act out and think you're proving a point. Do you know what that's called, Jamie? That's called pushing people away."

She had never yelled before. Actually, that probably wasn't true. More fair and accurate to say Jamie had never seen her yell before and honestly couldn't imagine that she ever had before tonight. The overhead, yellow light only illuminated half of her face but Jamie could see that tears were forming in her eyes. Small droplets of pain which Jamie had caused into being. They were unaccustomed to an emotional intertwine with so much at stake but their resolution to have their point heard remained strong.

Or sturdy at the very least.

"Caoimhe," they began. "I mean, after last time, I just had to let them know who I was and what I stood for. I felt like I owed that to myself."

"If you genuinely think that was some brazen display of self-respect, I feel bad for you. That whole show was a way for you to distance yourself from this situation. For you to feel like this young, queer icon you've always wanted to be. I mean, can't you see the obvious? It's right in front of you. You're growing up. I know it's faster than you intended and I know you don't think that you're ready but when you are a grown up, you don't waste time and effort on people who don't matter to you. You accept that they will have their horrible views because you have more important things to worry about."

"Caoimhe, they're your family."

"Exactly. They're my family. I have to deal with them and their crap. That's on me. They're not some obstacle for you to overcome or way for you to get your groove back. They don't matter."

Jamie was confused. It was as blatant as the makeup on their face.

"Oh, Jamie" said Caoimhe, sinking against a wall to sit on the dry ground. "Come down here for a minute."

Jamie complied, sat down next to her and took hold of her open hand.

"I'm going to tell you something, Jamie. I'm pretty scared. I'm scared about this baby and if it's going to be okay and I'm scared of whether or not those terrified people in there are going to be able to handle it, but the one thing I was never scared about is you. I knew from the first night we met, that you were someone I could rely on. The more we talked, the more I was sure and I don't care if you don't have a job yet because I know you'll get one. And I don't care if you're not what people will think of when I tell them about my baby's father. You're a beautiful, unique, miracle and I look forward to many years of surprising the unsuspecting public with you. The only thing I care about is that you recognise the reality of the situation and know that other people need you now."

"So, you think I'm selfish?"

"I didn't say that and I don't think it. I just think that you've lived your life like a work of art. It was all-consuming and very beautiful to you. You were willing to put up with a lot of abuse just so you could do things your way. I wish I had lived like that, even just once. Now, I'm not queer so I can't tell you what to do or when to defend yourself or express yourself or anything like that. I just want you to know that I'm scared but if you're scared too, you can talk to me about it."

The summer air was cool in this particular suburban back garden. Jamie's eyes were watering and the soft, warm feel of Caoimhe's hand was an anchor tethering them to earth, bound to the reality of the situation.

"I suppose I'm scared too," said Jamie. "I ... well, I guess I'm just scared that I won't be able to live the way I want or do the things I want or come and go as I please and I'm scared that this baby will…"

The words were caught in Jamie's throat.

"Ruin your life?" asked Caoimhe.

Jamie let out a small laugh in agreement as a tear ran down their cheek. "Hey, it's okay," she said. "You're definitely not the first young father to think that. You don't think that I felt that way? I had a full blown panic attack when I found out. Then, the more I thought about it, I realised that it's not a death sentence. Most of the great people in the world who ever did anything, did so with children. Also, I realised that I could become a person with responsibility who doesn't have to change who they are. That's what I want our child to see when they look at you. Not some straight passing shell like your last visit or someone looking to pick a fight to make themselves feel better. I want them to see someone living the best way they can with pride, dignity and all the flare you can muster. Frankly, I can't think of a better father figure."

Jamie didn't know what to say. How could anything they say compare to her? They had come here tonight searching for something explosive and cathartic. Instead, they were reduced to putty. Jamie was malleable in Caoimhe's hands and they loved it. Never before had they put so much faith and trust in one person, save perhaps for Akib.

She must have sensed their speechlessness as, instead of waiting for a response from Jamie, she took control of their hand.

"Here, try this," she said, placing Jamie's hand

under her T-shirt, onto her stomach and the thin membrane of nutrients between Jamie's past and their future. Feeling the delicate potential in front of them, the tight feeling in Jamie's upper shoulders began to dissipate. Instead of yelping with relief, they turned and stared deep into those beckoning pools of green before professing their future with those three words. Caoimhe smiled, responded in kind and kissed Jamie on the mouth. Jamie tasted the honey and felt the tingle from her body. She placed her free arm around them and Jamie felt small and protected.

They would both eventually have to go inside and face the night but right then, our two unlikely lovers sat and stared at the night sky. The motion-activated light had long since turned off, so the closer, larger stars were just about visible. Jamie thought of two things. The first was of how much some of the larger stars reminded them of Caoimhe. The second was of Ren and how Jamie had misinterpreted their words.

This is my birth right, thought Jamie, before sinking deeper into Caoimhe's arms.

Chapter 8

Wherein we
insist that we have
a pair, and that
somehow this
solves
everything.

(8)

"What do you mean, you're ace?" asked Barry.

"I'm asexual," answered Chentre. "Or on the asexual spectrum, I should say."

Several months had passed since Barry had attempted the great exodus from family life. The memory of the unmitigated failure of that night was a painful one but what hurt even more was how fast and obliviously things had returned to normal. Barry went to work, came home and sat with his wife and children. Even keeping the secret of his nocturnal trips to some of the city's more clandestine bars provided little excitement anymore. Barry was sure that Paulina knew he could not possibly be working late as often as he said but she refused to confront him about it. Instead, when he arrived home and climbed into bed at the outrageous time of four in the morning, she would simply kiss the back of his neck and welcome him home. On occasion, she would even have his lunch for the next day prepared, and uniform ironed.

What kind a sociopath was she? Barry would think during those sleepless nights.

Now, during another undercover mission, Barry was

speaking to Chentre, a handsome figure of broad shoulders who brought to mind a young Ricardo Montalbán.

"So, like, you don't have sex?" asked Barry in genuine bewilderment.

"Oh no, I've had sex before. A few times in the past. I never really get much out of it."

Didn't get much out of it? To Barry, this was obstinate to the point of being insulting. *Well, you must have done it wrong*, he thought. People don't get much out of a new appliance or playing golf, but sex was its own pursuit, goal and reward. How could this conventionally attractive person actually sit there and spout this heresy?

"So, you're just going to be alone forever?"

"I mean, that's a possibility for everyone on the planet, but I've had partners before."

"Oh, okay. So, like, other asexual people? Now it all makes sense."

"It's always made perfect sense to me and no, not just asexual people. I'm poly-romantic so if I choose to be with someone, I usually respond to the personality and sense of humour of any person. I just broke up with my last partner a few months ago and they were pansexual," said Chentre who was casually unaware that he was blowing Barry's mind.

"How can you be in a relationship with someone who wants to have sex when you have no interest?" asked Barry, completely missing the parallels with his own life. "Do you just close your eyes and get through it?"

This particular pub was known for a calm atmosphere. As such, there were no flashing lights and the music was at a restrained volume. This lack of stimulus only served to highlight the look of insult on Chentre's face at Barry's question. It would have been obvious to everyone in the room, save for Barry himself.

"You know, being in a relationship isn't everything. It's more important to know who you are and be comfortable with that. Plus, even if you are in a relationship, sex isn't everything. It is possible for two or more people to come together and share a life together. There are options outside the normal setup of two people coming together, going through the same three positions and then resenting each other over time. I've been in open relationships and polyamorous relationships and relationships where people were embracing an abstinent period in their life and I was happy in every one of them. I never had to close my eyes and get through anything except a few messy break ups." Any other person would have heard the displeased tone in Chentre's voice. Some may have even offered an apology. Barry simply pressed on. His questioning was not from curiosity but rather from a sneaking suspicion that this person may be lying.

"Okay, so I get that relationships can be weird for you and stuff but when you're alone you must, you know, with porn and stuff?"

The question hung in the air like rotten fruit.

"What is wrong with you?" asked Chentre.

"Hey, don't get mad at me just because you can't figure out what you want. Plus, if you really don't want to sleep with anyone, what brings you to a gay bar? This isn't exactly relationship city."

"Because it's a free country," was all the answer that Chentre cared to give.

Barry was bored. This conversation had reached its apex. Barry told himself it was because this person wasn't making sense and was obviously just making things up on the spot. Of course, the real reason was that Barry was inherently uninterested in people with whom he did not want to sleep. He and Chentre were polar opposites in that regard. Looking away to survey the room and its occupants, Barry spotted Ian, someone with whom he had had a previous dalliance half a year ago. He was standing at a small table, laughing with a group of similarly dressed men. That was where Barry wanted to be.

God, I wonder, is there a uniform or secret handshake for the clone club?

Turning back to the now silent Chentre, Barry spoke as he was standing up to leave. "I gotta go. This has been fun. I'll see you around sometime."

"I doubt that very much," was the last thing Barry heard as he moved toward Ian's table.

Approaching the table of patrons, all suited and booted in their best fitting trousers and plain, black T-Shirts, Barry felt a certain nervousness. It was unfamiliar and he liked it. How long could one go without a new experience to fire the synapses? If there was an answer,

Barry was sure that he had encountered it before and, although approaching a handsome man was no longer a brand new experience for Barry, he could not deny the youthful flutter in his stomach. He was, after all, only human.

Barry could hear Ian speaking to his peers before turning to face him. A bleached smile spread across his sunbed tan face. "No, I wouldn't go near him now. He's no fun ever since he got clean … Oh, if it isn't mystery man from before. It's Larry, right?" he asked.

"It's Barry actually and you're … Sean, right?"

"I can be if you like," said Ian with a laugh. "Come on, mystery man Barry. I was just going to pick up a drink. You can join me."

With that, Barry walked away from Ian's dull but gratifyingly mute friends and followed him to the bar. The bars lack of music and full lighting made the walk very obvious. Barry attempted a casual saunter before leaning against the bar. Ian half chuckled before ordering from the bar staff.

Ya, try to avoid punching any jukeboxes there, Fonzie, thought Barry.

"So, I saw you were talking to Mother Superior."

Barry thought for a second. "You mean Chentre?"

"That's right. We call him that because of his vow of chastity."

"He says he's on the asexual spectrum. I'm not sure there's anything ecclesiastical about it."

"Spectrum. Of course," said Ian. "Everyone is on a spectrum now. You can't just be one thing anymore. You have to lots of little things. When we were growing up, you were either straight or a homo. Normal or crazy. Now it's like everyone is a weird colour chart of a person."

A member of the bar staff returned with a red tinted cocktail. Ian promptly took a sip.

"Oh ya, I'm a no gender alien who hates their parents and also gluten and dairy will kill me," said Barry. The two shared an unashamed laugh.

Finally, thought Barry, *somebody normal to talk to.*

"Speaking of straights and homos, how are you doing, mystery man? Last I heard, you were still dancing the married man Macarena."

"It's true and it's almost as infuriating as the song. I've not really been able to think about anything else for the past few months. I feel like every night I come really close at least once and then a wave of nerves washes over me and I just lose it. It's frustrating."

"I bet it is but you have to stop whining about it. You sound like a girl right now."

Barry felt sufficiently chastised. "It's just that Paulina is sensitive and dependant on me financially. I'm not really sure what would happen to her or the kids."

"Kids? You never mentioned kids."

"Ya, I have two."

"Oh, you really are in it deep, my newly out friend. Wife, kids, a little mortgage and a cute little life. I bet you have fine china and towels that only guests can use and everything. Hell, you probably have even less fun than Mother Superior over there."

"I have a life, Ian. I don't live in a sitcom of clichés. It's just life. Like, it's my life. I never thought about it much until the last year or so."

"What changed?" asked Ian.

"I don't know," said Barry, thinking back. As far as he remembered, he had always had an attraction to men. He never actively repressed these inclinations. More accurate to say that he had managed to efficiently compartmentalise and, armed with this ability, Barry had resigned himself to the idea of a life well lived. Accordingly, he found a woman, married her and produced a manageable number of offspring. Looking back on it now, Barry viewed the entire endeavour with a clinical detachment as if his wedding vows, mortgage deposit and even his sperm had been coerced from him under fraudulent pretences. Then, one perfectly average Tuesday, Barry had decided that he had endured enough. Nothing of note had occurred. He had not had a recent birthday, nor had he been transfixed by a figure of beauty. If he had to guess, he would say that curiosity, deep instinctual curiosity, finally got the better of him. He remembered feeling excited at the prospect of starting over and was surprised at how peacefully he had reached the decision. For him, it was as easy as deciding not to finish an unpleasant meal. "I suppose nothing really changed. I'm just getting older."

"Ya, I think we're all aware of that. Your crow's feet look like they were made by ostriches. You should get those looked at. You could go to my guy up north. He does great work."

As Ian took another sip, Barry held a self-conscious hand to his temples. "You definitely aren't shy about stating your opinion."

"I'm not shy about anything, Barry. I'm loud, I'm proud and I can assure you that I if was trapped in this shell of a marriage you're describing, I'd be out of that house with a cosmo in my hand before she could yell *'Child Support Payments'*."

"Oh, you think it's that easy?" asked Barry.

Ian reached forward and tapped a finger against Barry's forehead. "You see, that's your problem, you're always think, think thinking. This isn't some kind of mission where you can avoid any pain if you do it just the right way. This is about you stepping up and growing a pair."

"Hey, I have a pair. You know that. I just want to wait until the time is right."

Ian choked on his drink as he laughed. Barry was sure it was done on purpose for dramatic purposes. "Wait until the time is right? I just have to believe that you don't even know what that means. You think your wife, ah, what did you call her, Paulina? Do you think Paulina is just going to come home one day, throw the good china and all your wedding photos in a fire and tell you to do what you want? Sorry, mister, but that is a fantasy and one that men have wasted their entire lives day-dreaming about for centuries."

Ian droned on. Not just on but on and on like a drone but not as gruesome and only half as politically volatile. Barry grew less and less focused with every smug, self-aggrandising word.

Do I hate this guy, or do I like him? he wondered.

The answer, you will be unsurprised to learn, was both. To Barry, someone like Ian represented not just the life he craved like an author craves a metaphor, but also a persona less dependent on the wellbeing of others. What bliss that life would bring! After all, Barry had always considered his compassion and consideration for the feelings of others to be his biggest flaw.

"Okay then, if you're so confident, what should I do? How do I broach that conversation in a way that will have an air of finality? I know you think it's just a matter of growing a pair or manning up or whatever, but I've been married for twelve years. It was something we built together and now I'm asking her … no, I'm telling her, that I want out. That's a tall order for any after-dinner conversation and I'm just a man."

Ian, who up to now had been a paragon of aloofness, took on a look that Barry almost suspected of indicating caring to some degree. Placing his drink on the bar, Ian reached out and placed both hands on Barry's shoulders, locking them both into an intensely private exchange. Being almost half a foot shorter than Ian, Barry could look up at his smooth, processed face. Tanned and groomed, Barry felt as though he was being held by a low-tier, soap-opera actor.

"Barry, you're not just a man, you're a <u>man</u>. You have power, you have strength. No one can tie you down if you don't want to. Look around this room. This is not just a gay bar full of ornery gentlemen. This is a room of men who have had to fight to be who they are. In this room alone, we probably have a few runaways, a handful of divorces and at least two complete abandonment of previous lives. If you think it's easy to be a gay man, I am here to dissuade you from that fantasy. The young people certainly have no idea what they are doing. The world has them so confused they don't know what they are, but we do. We're men and we take what we have to. So, if you want to sit your woman down for the last time and tell her that you're gone, you just do it. Use your power and get it done."

Emotionally speaking, Barry was simple. Donkey kick to the head, simple. Accordingly, this misogynistic, hollow and oddly repetitive speech made sense to him. Why shouldn't he barge in and tell Paulina exactly what he was going to do? What was stopping him now? He had an advantage over most men in his position in that he had already come out. Suddenly, the entire scenario seemed strange to him. He had been wanting something for so long now and he had done nothing to make it happen. That was not the way in which he was raised.

Granted, this is probably not what Dad had in mind.

Feeling flushed with energy, Barry grabbed hold of his beer. The smooth glass was cold against his hand and by the time the last of the teasing bubbles had passed his lips, he had conjured up the nerve to make his break for freedom. Had Paulina been sitting there with him, he would have turned and done the deed right there. As it stood, she was at home, ironing one of his shirts, taking the extra time to get the collar nice and stiff.

What great clarity this was. How could he have gone this long without any action? Knowing his time had come, Barry resolved to make tonight the night. He knew it was the right thing to do for all parties and nothing in the world would distract him.

"So, would you like to continue this conversation in a more private setting?" asked Ian.

Oh!

"You mean leave here together?"

"Yes," answered Ian, "but only on two conditions. The first is that we stay here for at least three more drinks because I'm not ready to call it a night yet, and the second is that we're finished talking about your wife. Deal?"

"A hard bargain but I suppose I could be persuaded to change the subject and order us another round."

"Good, I'm going to go re-join my group of friends. Come join us when you're ready."

Ian, having all the charm of an aristocratic simpleton, walked away, leaving Barry to order, purchase and carry the drinks on his own. He took no notice, of course. Barry's chest was tingling with excitement. The prospect of spending a night with Ian, coupled with his new wave of resolve, created a most pleasant angina, but also a flaw in his plans. Spending time with Ian in a more private setting would inevitably lead to arriving home in the late hours of the morning when Paulina would be long asleep. Also, though Ian had been very clear regarding his terms, Barry knew he would be completely unable to steer his thoughts and conversation away from himself.

The solution was clear. Paulina deserved a good night's sleep and would probably be more open to a difficult conversation tomorrow or even the day after. Much better for all concerned if he spent the night elsewhere.

Also, after a few drinks, Ian probably won't have much to say regarding the quality of conversation anyway, so no harm done there.

Continuing to lie to the only two adults in the world who showed him any affection was definitely a good idea. It would spare them both pain, for tonight at least.

As Barry carried two fresh drinks back to the crowded table with the clear, pre-meditated intent on violating his marriage vows, he could not help but feel pride in his selflessness.

Just as we thought, Barry. This compassion for others is leading us into trouble again.

Chapter 9

Wherein we give up control and receive chills of a not unpleasant nature.

(9)

"Never?" asked Dr Fallon.

"I wouldn't exactly say never," responded Orion. "I mean, there have been plenty of women to whom I've been really attracted. Mostly on TV and in movies and stuff."

"Any in real life?"

"Maybe one or two. Does that matter?"

"Orion, you know I don't ask you about things that don't matter. It's very natural for all of us to be attracted to film stars and models of any gender because of a degree of safety in the distance and how we would never have to confront our feelings or engage in any kind of relationship. What we're trying to establish here is whether or not you have ever felt the urge to seek further intimacy, in person, with anyone who wasn't a man."

"Jesus, you're starting to sound like some gay conversion counsellor," said Orion with instant regret.

Dr Fallon, being a professional, retained a neutral expression but Orion could see that his last comment had caused hurt. Feeling very small, he chose not to apologise and, instead, accept the admonishment of her stern tone.

"That is not what is happening here, Orion. I am just trying to talk to you about something you've brought up many times which is your sexuality and how you feel it can limit you in different ways."

Sitting just as he was now, in one of Dr Fallon's comfy armchairs, Orion had discussed the topic often but present memory drew him back to the first time. After his night out with Sarah.

Sarah, a friend of sunny disposition, was rarely seen without her notoriously jealous boyfriend, Rob. Such was the degree of notoriety, that on more than one occasion, Orion had witnessed Rob intentionally secluding Sarah from some of her male friends. This level of control made Orion uncomfortable and so, he was dreading a night out with Sarah. To his surprise, however, Rob was a perfect gentleman. He never reared his head when Sarah and Orion were enjoying drinks together. He never interrupted while they danced together. Finally, at the end of the night, he even thanked Orion with a friendly hug.

It didn't take Orion long to deduce the reason for Rob's sudden, enlightened behaviour. Rob didn't see Orion as a threat because Orion was gay. Essentially, Orion had been made a eunuch. The expectations of him were clear. He was to prepare Sarah with alcohol, entertain her with dancing and then, at the end of the night, hand her back to her boyfriend. Most importantly, he was to do all of this without a hint of sexuality. He was to keep his preclusions within his gender and never wander outside.

Orion was gorgeous. He was strong, charming and fun to be around in the right setting but all of this was insignificant to Rob who had reduced Orion to the position of a sexless clown. A strange, Teflon semi-man who posed no threat and was unworthy of even a hint of his trademark jealousy. Suffice to say, this rubbed Orion the wrong way.

During one session, bearing the full and bruised fruit of male machismo, Orion sat and divulged these events to Dr Fallon and, while she was quick to remind him that his feelings were stemming from outdated and unnecessary notions of male pride, the topic of Orion's sexuality, and what it means to him, had been on the table ever since.

Dr Fallon, perhaps seeing that Orion was feeling suitably admonished, adopted her regular warm tone. "Look, it's obvious that you don't want to discuss this at the moment and that's fine. I just want you to remember what we've discussed in the past; about how you occasionally can feel trapped in the image that you've crafted of yourself. I feel like being young and finding yourself attracted to men, you naturally assumed the identity of a gay man, but from our sessions, I also feel like part of you is rebelling from that narrow view and the lack of acting on it is causing you some distress. Anyway, putting that aside for the moment, I think we should review the exercises I suggested last—"

"I get jealous sometimes," interrupted Orion. "Sorry, but I do get jealous. There are so many different people and different kinds of people and genders and preferences and it just seems like this whole new exciting world. Then you have me and I'm just sticking to men which is this singular thing and I just feel uncomfortable pursuing anyone else. I dunno, I guess it makes me feel safe but definitely when I see someone that I find attractive and they may not be exactly what I'm used to, I get jealous and frustrated that I feel unable to do anything or even really contemplate it."

"Orion, are the feelings you have toward these people identical to the feelings of attraction you have toward men?"

"Not quite. I feel it might be similar to what you were saying earlier about celebrities. I feel attraction but there's definitely distance, like a woman or non-binary person that I like is somehow unattainable so it's okay for me to feel this way because it will never happen anyway."

Orion thought back to his last relationship or more accurately, he thought about the distance between that point and his present. Three years had passed since that last coupling. Orion, painfully aware of the little success his dating life had wrought in that time, suddenly felt sad. He imagined dark and heavy rain outside the non-window on the wall to his right. "But I'm not ready for this at the moment. Can we talk about something else?"

"We can talk about anything you want, Orion. You know that" said Dr Fallon, emphatically taking her tablet and placing it on the table to her side. Orion had noted that she did this when she wanted to appear non-clinical. He appreciated the gesture. "So, how are your preparations for the contest?"

"Pretty good," he answered. "I don't like to think of

it as a contest, though. More like a showcase. I have some great gear ready."

"And the interview and talent sections that you've told me about?"

"The interview and talent section, yes. I know in the past I've had trouble with crowds or public settings but when I think of standing in front of that crowd or the other people onstage, I don't feel nervous. I've been thinking about it a lot actually, as you can imagine, and I'm still not sure why that is. What do you think?"

"Good question," she said, holding her warm mug with both hands. "In the past we've discussed how your anxiety can be linked to your perception of people's awareness of you in social settings but when you're on stage or talking to a crowd, people's attention is definitely on you. Your perception of their awareness of you is less distorted due to your certainty of the situation. It's not uncommon. Many famous performers of all kinds experience anxiety. Performing is a way in which you can control a room and its occupants in a way which is healthy and utilises a creative outlet."

"But is that a healthy mindset?" he asked. "Constantly wanting to control people and needing to be the centre of attention in order to feel safe."

"Like I said, I think it's control in a healthy setting. You're not looking to hurt or oppress anyone. You're just creating a scenario wherein you feel in control of your own actions and the way in which people see you. People do it all the time with humour or other aspects of their personality. What is important for us is that we need to marry those to aspects of yourself. The one that feels like they'd be safe and comfortable on stage and the one that lives his life in normal everyday settings. Tell me, how do you feel when you're in gear and with other people?"

Orion thought back to his younger self and his first pair of Doc Martens. The leather was sturdy and smooth. When he slid the hungry, dark, 20-eyelet mouths onto his feet and pulled the white laces tight, he did not just feel different. He was different. "I suppose I feel relaxed. I feel strong. I feel sexy and I feel like I'm taking a small vacation from myself. There's a liberating pleasure in spending your nights doing something that you wouldn't discuss with your parents. It's a small thrill but it accumulates over time and suddenly you feel okay being exposed in ways you wouldn't have, otherwise."

Orion looked to his right and noticed that the imaginary rain had stopped. Grey clouds remained but they were faltering, surely under the persistence of a beautifully intrusive sun.

"When I put on my gear, I feel free."

Orion was standing at a table in the main room of a local queer resource centre, the very same one that had housed the first meeting among contestants and would be the same to house the Alt-Gear showcase in just over a month. To further facilitate interaction between contestants, the organisers had rented the centre at several intervals. Contestants and friends were encouraged to attend and share ideas.

Orion stood alone.

It didn't bother him, though. There was a quiet tranquillity in the ability to stand alone in a crowded room. Scribbling on a page titled *Talent Section,* he felt no pressure or animosity from the room's occupants. Dressed casually in a white T-shirt and a Rob of Amsterdam bartender waistcoat with double white stripes, Orion enjoyed the security he had described to Dr Fallon the previous day.

A small group to Orion's left consisted of Chandra, Goddess Kira and two people with whom Orion was not familiar. Hoping to concentrate on his work, Orion moved across the room from his solitary table to his bag to retrieve a fresh pen. As he did so, his orbit was interrupted, and he was pulled in by nearby conversation.

"Oh no, I'm number Ten all the way," said Chandra. "I mean, I don't want to fan-girl out too much, but the look and the humour and the whole Romantic Byronesque figure was so on point plus, I think he had the best stories. Golden Age Davies' stuff. Like, we got *The Sound of Drums* and *The Last of the Timelords*. Plus, we had Martha, the best companion."

"Martha? I think you mean Donna. Everyone loves a spicy redhead," said Goddess Kira.

"Hey, I'm not saying anything bad about Donna. I just think Martha is underrated. I would go far as to say criminally underrated."

"Well then, lock me up, you mischievous pup because it's the Doctor Donna for me."

The small group laughed as Chandra, playful as ever, mimed placing Goddess Kira in handcuffs in preparation to stand trial for crimes against science fiction.

Goddess Kira had noticed Orion half hovering nearby. "Oh, Orion, who's your favourite Doctor?"

He didn't need to think. To him it was a fun question but one that required an obvious answer. "Twelve," he said with confidence.

"Twelve!" exclaimed Chandra. "There's few good episodes there for sure but I think Twelve brought everything down. It was like watching a star burn out."

"Bad puppy!" said Orion with a smile. "Twelve was the most professional. He had a mission and he stuck to it. Plus, I loved his whole look and persona. He acted like he was in some punk band during the Thatcher years. All the rest of the band are dead and he's just older with more money and energy than he knows what to do with so he just travels around adventuring, saving people and scaring the crap out of anyone who stands in his way."

"That actually does sound pretty punk," said Goddess Kira.

"I guess we don't have to agree as long as we all think Captain Jack is the alien-fighting, pansexual hero the world needs right now," said Chandra. "Hey, I'm gonna step out for twenty and grab some grub before heading back. You guys in?"

"I think I'm just going to stay for the moment and

keep working," said Orion.

"I'm going to stick around here as well. I'll be here when you get back though," said Goddess Kira.

With that, Pup Chandra and the two others walked away in search of food. Orion waited until she was out of earshot before leaning toward Goddess Kira. "I actually always found Gwen to be the best part of Torchwood."

Goddess Kira's eyes grew wide as they stifled back a nasal laugh. "Oh my God, same, but I wouldn't have said that to Chandra. She's a scrappy puppy."

Orion, not able to think of anything else to say, simply leaned back toward his table. His green-haired, gothic goddess companion, dressed opulently in a lace-up leather-skirted corset dress and thigh-high boots, joined him in his movements. "So, what are you working on?" they asked.

"Uh, it's just a list of ideas for the talent section. Still not quite sure what I'm going to do," he said while folding his page in two.

"Don't stress about it too much," they said. "Most people aren't too sure either. Personally, I like it when you leave it to the last minute. Makes for some fun and messy talents. Then again, the judges might have a different opinion. I'm just one of the organisers after all. Speaking of which, if you have any questions about anything, please let me know."

Unbeknownst to Orion, who was occupied trying to think of the most subtle way in which to place the folded page into his pocket without seeming rude, Goddess Kira had moved several inches closer. Their lips, adorned with black lipstick, were in the form of a coy smile.

"Actually, there is one thing I've wanted to ask you, Kira."

"Ah, it's Goddess or Goddess Kira, actually," they said, never losing that smile.

Orion was slightly taken back. "Sorry, of course. Goddess, why is this known as the alternative gear contest? When you set it up with Benny, what were your intentions in terms of it being alternative?"

"That's a great question. When we first wanted to set up our own contest, we wanted it to be inclusive. Like, really inclusive. I mean, when you think of a BDSM gear event, the first image that comes to mind is big, leather men with cigars and muir caps."

"Doesn't sound so bad to me," said Orion, thinking about the eagle-pin muir cap in his bedroom cupboard.

"Oh, definitely. I mean, there's nothing wrong with that. I always said that if I had control of a TARDIS, I would go back to a leather scene somewhere in Berlin or New York in the 80s. I'd love to see those men living in a way which must have seemed odd but also so comfortable to them. I like to think there would be this prevailing sense of danger but also a sense that what they were doing was blazing a trail for sexual liberation."

"Sounds a bit more like a Torchwood episode to me," quipped Orion.

Another nasal laugh from Goddess Kira made Orion smile. "Oh, that's actually your laugh. I thought you were being sarcastic earlier."

A third laugh now, even more adorably distorted than the first two. "I can't help it. I'd do something about it but I love to laugh, and it seems to make people happy."

"Is that a Goddesses job? To make people happy?"

"Why, Orion, my gloomy friend, that's what this is all about. Making each other happy, whether you hold the leash or wear the collar."

Their eyes met for a second. Orion noticed that theirs matched their hair. He also noted that they were staring at him for some reason. Perhaps he had something on his face or maybe this silent pause had gone on too long. "So, you were talking about the alternative aspect of all of this, Goddess?"

"Ya, so, when Benny and I decided we wanted to set up our own event, we wanted to imbue it with a different aura. We don't think we're better or more progressive or anything, we just wanted to make sure that as many different types of people felt as welcome as possible. After a little research, we found that the best way to do that was to work the word alternative in there somewhere. Now, I know what you're thinking. If we label ourselves as alternative, then aren't we making ourselves seem odd or exotic in some way? That was a risk, but we decided to take it. Plus, I think it's been a success so far and I'm super happy to have made any tiny contribution to our little local queer culture."

That was a phrase Orion had never fully understood. "What do you think Queer Culture is exactly?" he asked.

"Oh," they said, slightly taken back, "I suppose that

technically Queer Culture is the collective art, social movements, events, and characteristics common to a majority of queer people. That's definitely a textbook though and probably doesn't answer your question. Um, I suppose that to me, Queer Culture is about the future while at the same time, insisting that we do have a past, no matter how hard some people would like to insist otherwise. I mean, I think it's a small bit about rebellion and I also think there's a really cool transhumanist aspect to it like we're evolving beyond old concepts left over from hunter-gatherer days, like monogamy and gender stereotypes. All of that is a little anthropological though. Sometimes it's just about art presented in a more subversive way than you'd expect. Do you know the song *Under Pressure*?"

"By Queen and Bowie?"

"Absolutely. Both parties are huge queer icons in their own right and it's a great song but the best version I've ever seen was by Veda."

Orion, not knowing if he should know who or what that was, raised his eyebrows in minor bewilderment.

"Oh, you don't know Veda?" they asked. "Veda is a drag queen and she is amazing. She's released a few albums and she was also in Daddy's Little Princess and LadyFace. I've seen her live numerous times but my favourite thing of hers is her rendition of *Under Pressure*."

Goddess Kira moved to Orion's left. As they did, they turned Orion away from the table so they both faced toward the wide, mostly empty room. Goddess Kira raised an arm to an invisible spectacle.

"Imagine that you're in a gay bar. It's a regular night so there's not much going on. Mostly just people looking for a little fun. Then, the stage lights up. Just a bit at first but enough to get everyone's attention. Then, slowly, the lights become brighter and brighter until the stage is fully lit. The music has turned off and everyone is looking centre stage, wondering what's happening. Then, finally, down descends a figure – tall, statuesque, almost demon-like in appearance and on the minimal side of glamorous. Dressed in white and black, her outfit cuts under her right arm, leaving her shoulder exposed. Above that, her hair is a crimson red and stands stiff and upright like the headpiece to some modern, Celtic priestess. The audience are transfixed as Veda, blessed with vascular magnetism, moves back toward a descending backdrop projection screen. A few more seconds of silence and then the music starts. Those first few beats of the song are pretty recognisable, so everyone starts cheering. Colours are projected on the backdrop and Veda moves and dips her hip to the beat. Then, as Bowie and Freddie come in with those opening lyrics, the stage comes alive. The backdrop that was just come colours, is suddenly full of Veda. Four, six or even eight projections, filmed previously in some professional shoot, all dancing and synching with lyrics. Then, made all the more real by her two-dimensional back-up doppelgangers, the real Veda is drawing everyone in. Every move and every step. Every click and clap. Every smile and snarl. Every time she opens her arms, more and more of the audience are drawn in and as the song goes on, the phantom images from the projector are writhing across her pale skin. Veda becomes this joyous canvas for her own art. She stomps and marches and throws her head from side to side, channelling the lyrics until we're at the end, except we're not the same audience we were at the beginning."

Orion stared at the empty space in front of him. With Goddess Kira's description, he couldn't help but feel he was there in the neon light glow of a transcendent drag performance. "Wow, you really have a way with description. Do you work in advertising or something?"

"Nah, I just have a great memory for things that I care about."

"So, do you ever perform live?"

"Life is a performance, Orion, and you're always centre stage."

For the second time in this conversation, their eyes met. Him, wondering what exactly they were looking at, and them thinking that Orion was cute but obviously not interested. Eventually, Goddess Kira decided on a tactical retreat. "So, I better let you get back to what you're working on. I'm sure it will be great. Oh, by the way, we've set up a group chat for everyone here. I'd love to add you, if you want. You want to give me your number?"

Oh, great, a group chat. If I wasn't nervous enough, now, I'll probably get sneak peeks at everyone's great ideas Still, must be social, thought Orion.

After securing Orion's number, Goddess Kira,

secure in their efforts, thought to cement their intentions. "I'll probably give you a message sometime. See if you ever want to do anything. Maybe I could even commit you to memory, if you'd like."

With that, they turned and walked away.

A few seconds passed and then a few seconds more. *They were flirting with me!*

Orion's eyes grew wide and his pulse grew faster. *No,* he thought. *This isn't the time. This is about a new hobby and meeting new people, not about giving out numbers and oddly sensual recanting of drag performances.*

Still, they had his number. He had given it up freely and in doing so, had placed the power in their corner. The idea gave him not-unpleasant chills.

Leaving soon thereafter and walking home, Orion was beset by thoughts. He thought about the contest, he thought about his talent section and, not unsurprisingly, he thought about Goddess Kira. Orion, with all his progressive ideals, could not deny that they were different from the people in which he usually took an interest. Still, he admired them and their forcefulness. It was brazen in a way that he found attractive. These thoughts, and similar others, rolled on throughout the night. Lying in bed, Orion decided to compartmentalise and store them away for further contemplation. After all, Goddess Kira was interesting in the best possible way but, after weighing up the possible outcomes, Orion couldn't help but doubt that anything would come from their conversation.

Chapter 10

Wherein we come a long way from that bathroom stall.

(10)

"So, ya. We've been going out for just over three weeks now," said Orion.

This was to be Orion's last session with Dr Fallon before the showcase and, as such, it was difficult for him to deny the air of finality in the room. Of course, he knew that was just semi-wishful thinking. Orion felt no animosity toward the prospect of his future presence in the sparse but inviting office. On the contrary, Orion had grown to view Dr Fallon for what she was: a dedicated professional who had worked hard to create an environment wherein Orion could help himself. The showcase, for example, was not her idea but he knew that he would not have been able to enter, let alone participate, without her help.

"They called me and the more we talked, the closer we got and I have to say that now, I'm pretty happy. I mean, it's really early but I think they're really cool and very strong in a way I think is fantastic."

"Orion, I'm very happy for you," said Dr Fallon with a familiar warmth. "I can tell that you're obviously quite smitten and it's adorable, but I also think this represents great progress for you. I do have to clarify, though; do they really go by *Goddess*?"

"It started as a scene name, but they just stuck with

it over time. I have to say that I kinda like it. When I tell someone, it creates this little pause when they're trying to process it and when I'm asked to clarify, I usually refuse. It's fun. Plus, they don't go around insisting that everyone and all their friends call them a Goddess. I just call them Kira, most of the time."

Dr Fallon looked up from her tablet. Orion could see that she had picked up on the not so subtle subtext. "<u>Most</u> of the time?" she asked. Orion nodded in response. "Orion," she began, "you've spoken in the past about your sexual persona and how you feel the way people treat you can derive from their interpretation of race and masculinity. Basically, you've often spoken about how it was consistently unfair that you were expected to take a dominant, masculine persona in intimate relationships."

"I have a vague recollection of that incredibly intimate conversation, yes."

"So, how do you feel your new relationship with Goddess Kira fits into that concern?"

"Obviously it's new and we're still working out the kinks, if you'll pardon the terrible pun, but one of the things I like most about Kira is that I never feel like I have to be something I'm not to make them happy and without resulting to scandalous imagery, I've been able to explore more aspects of my sexuality than ever before. With Kira, I'm able to adopt different personas and whether that's one of submission or dominance or involving different people or body types than what I'm used to, I feel very safe and very excited."

"Orion, I feel like that's tremendous progress in terms of the concerns you've raised previously, and I look forward to discussing your evolving knowledge of yourself in subsequent sessions. Now, we have only two minutes left but at this point, I feel like I would be remiss if I didn't ask you your feelings in relation to pursuing a relationship with someone who identifies as non-binary."

Orion should have seen this question coming, especially in light of his previous comments about feeling trapped in a purely male-centric dating pool.

"I did not seek it out, both being in a relationship or the non-binary aspect. I'm not the guy who goes out and chooses to be with someone just because they're nature is trendy or subversive in some way. Those people are users and that's not me. I will admit that I did think about it a bit before our first date. Truth be told, I thought about cancelling but then I thought about you and some of the stuff we've discussed here, and I realised that was just fear. Fear of being judged or a fear of standing out in some way. So, I went ahead with the date and as soon as our personalities started clicking, none of it seemed to matter anymore."

"So, you felt that you were able to forget that they were non-binary after a while?" she asked.

"No, not really but I didn't want to forget. I think that would be doing Kira a disservice if I was trying to forget or deny that they were who they were just so I could be with them. I suppose it's complex and it's true, I don't really think about them being non-binary anymore, but I also never want to forget that they are a proud, wild, beautiful, strong non-binary person who has fought to be who they are. Frankly, I look forward to a long time of responding to awkward misgenderings with them."

Orion looked to his right, to his usual spot, except this time, he sought no escapism. The wall to his side was not possessed by phantom rain or sun. There were no storms or birds. No pedestrians or cars. There was not even a sky. To Orion's right there was a wall. It was blue, bare and sturdy. Its presence produced no reaction, emotional or otherwise, and the world beyond its dimensions was a benign mystery. The edges of Orion's mouth curved to a smile as he turned back to Dr Fallon. "I suppose I'm just not that scared anymore."

They both knew that his statement was significant but lacked permanency. Relapse and re-admission were part of the healing process. Still, Dr Fallon could not help but feel a sense of pride. "Orion, I'm very happy to hear you say that. I think this has been one of our better sessions and I so look forward to continuing this momentum next time."

Orion nodded and stood up to leave. He could not help but think back to leaving his first session when he was filled with scepticism. After all, how could therapy help relieve the anxiety of someone so unique and complex as he? Months later and he was transformed. Could he really leave without saying anything? Choosing to err on the side of sentimentality, he turned back to the good doctor.

"Angela, I know that you're a professional, but I just wanted to say thank you. When I came here, I wasn't even aware of how many things were causing me distress and now, after our time together, I'm able to do and be so much more. I don't know where I'd be right now without you."

She was a professional but still human and so, very human tears began to form in her eyes as her Orion, just now setting out on a journey of discovery, expressed his gratitude. "You're very welcome, Orion. Good luck at your showcase and I look forward to hearing all about it."

With that, he smiled, turned and exited the office. He knew that his objective should be to work through the necessity of these visits and leave the treatment behind. He both dreaded and desired that day. For now, as he walked down the corridor to schedule his next session with Dr Fallon's receptionist, Orion felt no trepidation and no anxiety. Instead, he was filled with a mix of gratitude and a resolution to live with curiosity and boldness. This was her gift to him. After months of care and patience, she had imparted onto him something very precious. He was strong and he was weak. He was dominant and he was submissive. He was a lover to all people now and their abstract joys and sorrows would be theirs and theirs alone.

Through celebration and the carefully constructed wax wings of hope, he had grown and had become more than what he was.

*****

Orion, along with the other participants, sat in a small room to the side of a makeshift stage. Contest or not, the event exuded a great air of informality. This was unsurprising to Orion as it would be short-sighted of any event organiser to enforce strict rules and procedures on an event hall full of people dressed in fetish gear. In terms of the variety and selection of gear, the crowd did not disappoint.

Before coming to cast a curious eye on his fellow participants, Orion was greeted by the multi-coloured, multi-textured, multi-persona and multi-species creations of the crowd. A pleasant, albeit muffled gimp in reflective rubber greeted him at the front entrance and showed him to the already full cloakroom and changing area. From there, he noticed that the hired security (who was performing the job for free as he was a friend to the community) surveyed and patrolled in a blue, leather, police-style shirt complete with Aviator glasses, handcuffs and gloves.

Orion had then been greeted by Goddess Kira who was speaking among a crowd of people who had followed their lead and embraced a BDSM goth aesthetic. They spoke only for a moment as Orion knew they both had work to do.

People walked, crawled and hobbled their way into the small room. Orion had joined in and spoken to almost all of them. The talk, as to be expected, was mostly shop talk.

"Where did you get this?"

"How much was that?"

"How can you breathe in that thing?"

Common questions. Now, as Orion worked calmly into his first look of the evening, the room was filled mostly with other participants as well as a few welcome additions. A yellow Pup Rolo stood brazenly in the corner with an adorable black and white Pup Blondie. Handler Chris, a muscled creature of mohawked magnetism, was also present.

Orion could hear the music from the main hall. Assuming the crowd would be at a healthy size, he ventured out for a look. Before he did so, he stopped to survey his work in the nearby full-length mirror. His first look of the night was relatively pedestrian by local standards. Standing firm in his leather patrol boots, Orion was sporting a pair of Rob of Amsterdam slim-fit leather pants with a white stripe. Above the waist, he wore a simple white T-shirt along with a black, leather Sam Browne that ran from his left hip and over his right shoulder. Knowing that accessories were the key to any ensemble, he had included a leather wrist wallet with white trim, a small silver neck chain with matching padlock and, finally, a dark muir cap with white piping. Orion took a vain, but very human, extra second to tense his biceps in the mirror before walking out to the main floor.

What he saw was not unfamiliar to anyone who had been on a night out, save for the preponderance of leather, latex, rubber, lace, chains and other assorted materials. He also couldn't help but feel pride in his relative ease. In the past, a crowd of this size would give rise in him, great feelings of envy. Instead, as he looked over this odd crowd of miscreants, of which he considered himself a proud member, Orion felt as though he could ask a hundred questions and still ask a hundred more.

Across the room, he spotted Goddess Kira who was chatting to an older gentleman. From their formal and informative body language, he may have been a sponsor of tonight's event. During the day, he was most likely a consummate professional. Every facet of his persona would be groomed and repressed in the most profitable way possible. Now, as he stood among a crowd of societies' dark enthusiasts, he was set free.

Kira flashed Orion a smile and a wave. He returned in kind and looked forward to speaking to them later.

Continuing to survey the room Orion spotted many familiar faces, including Jamie and Akib. Akib, with whom Orion was only partly familiar, was sipping from a glass tumbler of unknown content while Jamie seemed to be holding a half-full bottle of water.

Perhaps their little kidneys finally gave in, thought Orion.

Catching Jamie's eye, Orion gestured a big wave and a smile. He was very much looking forward to speaking to Jamie later in the evening, partly for the pleasure of a familiar face but also because he had recently heard some rumour about Jamie that he wanted to discredit.

Satisfied, Orion returned to the stage-side dressing room. There was a holy cacophony of zips, straps, buttons, buckles, locks and clasps as people prepared themselves. At this point, the order of the evening was known to everyone. All contestants would be wearing two outfits for the night. The first, the more casual of the two, would be worn during the first stage which was the interview stage. Goddess Kira had explained to Orion that *interview* may have been something of a grandiose term as the interchange would consist of only one question to be answered on the spot, in front of the audience, with no preparation.

The second stage of the night would consist of all contestants displaying their second outfit, on stage, to a soundtrack of their choice. Orion had already submitted his soundtrack and the components of his second outfit lay in waiting in a small, dark blue suitcase.

The last stage of the night would be one where each contestant would be asked to display a talent. The judges, themselves a grouping of open-minded kinksters, would be awarding extra points for originality. Shortly after this, the judges would confer, and a winner would be announced to the crowd.

Goddess Kira entered the room, filled with the type-A productive energy of someone with an event to keep on track. "Hey, you," they said, pausing to plant an excitable kiss on Orion.

"I'm good. Feeling strong. Feeling ready."

"Good! I love it, I love it, I love it. I hope everyone shares your enthusiasm because we're going to start up in a few minutes."

Goddess Kira turned to address the room. "Hi, everyone. Oh, my great gothic God, don't you all look fantastic. I've been helping organise this event for a while now and every year, including this year, is always so fantastic when I get to see what people bring to the table. And this is just your first outfit! I can't wait to see what you all have planned for the second stage. Anyway, we're going to be starting soon. What's going to happen is the music will stop and you'll be called out, one by one, in the order you've already been given. The crowd will cheer because they're amazing and so are you and then Benny the host will ask you your question. Remember, this is not a government inquiry. The questions will be totally open to interpretation. You can make your answers as long as you want. You can even answer in the form of interpretive dance, if that's where you are at the moment. All that matters is that you answer honestly and have fun. If you've any problems, I'll be right out there; feel free to find me or stare right at me if that helps centre you while you're on stage. Good luck, everyone, let's give 'em a good show."

With that, Goddess Kira gave Orion a kiss and left the room, pausing only to scratch an eager rubber pup behind the ear.

The alternative kink showcase, something Orion first learned about several months ago in the harsh afterglow of an anxiety induced panic attack, had finally begun. Orion hadn't lied to Goddess Kira. He felt ready.

Time passed and several contestants had exited the

room, only to return after presenting their look and answer to the audience. Orion, and everyone else, stood close to the door so as to hear them. Goddess Kira had not been overstating when they assured the room of the crowd's ability to cheer. So far, every contestant had been welcomed onstage with an enthusiastic reception. Each question asked had been different but retained a degree of similarity.

Pup Chandra was just now returning from the stage. Her first outfit of the night consisted mainly of a Regulation K9 ¾ rubber suit in blue, accessorised with a Mr S neoprene collar. The reception from the crowd was still audible as, when asked her interview question, Chandra spoke so passionately about community, creativity and the value of proper gear maintenance, that grown men wept. Sauntering back into the room, Chandra emptied the contents of a bottle of water in one gulp and then set to work on her second outfit of the night. She was truly a good puppy.

Up next and already ascending the stage, was Keith. Months ago, at the meet and greet, Keith had spoken about meeting their partner in depressing but self-actualising circumstances. Armed with a determination that Orion could recognise, Keith had spent the time between then and now using the creativity awarded from the fetish community to grow. The change was obvious and glorious. Instead of the somewhat anonymous figure of handsome features that Orion had met, Keith stood tall in the 6-inch heels of his calf-length, latex boots. Covering their entire body below the neck, he wore a black Sealwear catsuit so well fitting that Orion assumed it had to be custom made. His hair, originally cut short, had grown over several months but was currently worn slick and brushed back. Additionally, he had added a patch of pink to his natural jet black. The entire look was clean, dark, sleek and all-encompassing. What mystery lay behind that eternal dark material? After receiving Keith's answer to their question, Benny the host dared to speak on behalf of the crowd.

"Keith, I have to ask because I know we're all looking at you and wondering, can you give us a little tease of your second outfit of the night?"

With that, Keith took two steps toward the crowd, raised the microphone and opened their mouth to speak before smiling, turning and walking off the stage.

The crowd erupted into applause and Keith re-entered the back room with a smile before setting to work on his second outfit.

Up next, and directly before Orion, was Aleksander, the Polish kinkster who had been embraced by the Berlin leather scene. This influence was very present in their first outfit of the night. Aleksander was sporting a pair of leather trousers with a red stripe running down the side, 12-eyelet Doc Marten boots with red laces and a Regulation leather polo shirt in red with black piping. Orion appreciated the classic look, even more so when he spotted a red handkerchief hanging from the back, right pocket of Aleksander's leather trousers.

Orion stood close to the doorway and listened. After the reassuringly loud reception from the crowd had died down, Benny took control of the room.

"Aleksander, it's great to see you and I think it's safe to say that the audience are a fan of your look. Now, as we well know, you have experience from scenes all around central Europe. With that experience, what would you say to someone who was interested in the gear scene but who felt intimidated by some of the more hardcore looks?"

Aleksander, always cool, drew a deep breath and answered as though he had given this advice before.

"I would tell them that they're definitely in the right place. One of the great things I've always found in the fetish gear scene was our ability and our mission to take power away from negative and potentially hurtful imagery and symbols. Someone once told me that they didn't like the scene because some of the people appeared as though they were trying to look like Nazis. When I asked him what he meant, he mentioned the boots and the muir caps and the leather coats and lots of the military gear. I told him that I thought it was a fantastic thing. In the past, when people saw a Nazi dressed up in his evil finery, they would rightfully be scared of this terrifying thing and from that fear, he would gain his power. Now, we have taken that power away. When I see someone dressed in their dark, intimidating military gear, I don't think that it's a dangerous person who's looking for my fear, I think that it's someone trying out their new boots. I wonder where they got their gloves. I wonder what kind of polish they're using. The last thing I do is fear them because I see no power left in their imagery. No malice in their symbols. We have taken all that and we have changed it. The same, I would say, is true for skinheads. In the 80s when the skinhead movement was infiltrated by racists, that image was implanted in people's heads until recent times. We have worked hard in co-opting the look and fashion of the racist skinhead persona for our own peaceful, creative purposes. So much imagery that we now associate with negative connotations, were stolen. Swastikas were originally religious symbols in Eurasia while the skinhead look originated from working class groups youth influenced by reggae and other foreign musical groups. When groups took this imagery and used it for their own evil goals and forced negative connotations on us, they stole something from all mankind. In a way, no matter how extinct or defeated they are, they still have control over our minds and our assumptions. Well, I say no to that. I'm proud to be part of a community which takes back what is rightfully ours and where people, all people, can form looks as hardcore as they want as long as they come from a place of diversity and compassion. So, to answer your question, I would advise that person, so intimidated by our looks and crowds, to embrace their fear and join the fight, embrace diversity, be creative and help take back what is rightfully theirs."

Orion and everyone in the back room within earshot joined in with the audience's applause. When Aleksander returned from the stage, Orion and several other contestants, greeted him with their congratulations.

Orion knew he was up next. He knew that most of the audience would be familiar to him and hoped that the strangers would be kind. Hearing his name and feeling proud to follow someone like Aleksander, Orion left the back room and stepped out to the centre stage.

The lights were soft, the crowd was welcoming and his anxiety was only spiking to a degree that Orion convinced himself was normal for anyone on stage. Encouraged by their reception, Orion smiled and waved to the crowd of misfits in front of him. From there he could see the familiar faces that he craved. Benny, the hunky host, took Orion by the shoulder and displayed him to the crowd. Their volume increased.

"Orion, I think it's safe to say that they approve," said Benny, talking over the crowd. "As you know, we don't do tacky introductions here like we're strangers on a gameshow. Instead, we get to understand people that we already know and in order to do that, we ask questions for which the contestants have had no preparation. The question that the judges have written for you is as follows: Orion, you've been very vocal about how relatively new you are to the scene and how much you've enjoyed it. For people who are just starting off, can you explain if and how being in the scene has changed you in just a few months?"

Orion hadn't been sure what to expect. The nature of the question was to make one think on the spot but, for Orion, this answer required no brain power. He had thought about little else for the past eight months. He watched and observed as, little by little, he had grown into his current state. Determined to stick to the spirit of the contest and what it meant to him, Orion took a deep breath and spoke honestly to his new friends.

"I never felt that I needed anyone, or at least I had convinced myself that I didn't need anyone else because people only brought small traumas and annoyances. With every comment and assumption, they would box me further and further into myself. After a while, it's easy for anyone in that position to feel trapped and helpless. That feeling came to a head several months ago when I went through a small traumatic event and started feeling probably the lowest I ever have. Then, for no reason other than a vague interest, I did something I don't usually do. I took a risk and tried something new. I didn't know it on my first meet up, but I was about to go through a serious and unconventional therapy technique. After all, what else could someone do other than grow in such a nurturing environment? What could I do but embrace my creative side when sharing ideas with such brave people? How could I not push and surprise myself when working with such talented competition? How could I not find harmony, bravery and even someone to care about when I was in such dark, beautiful, instinctual and wild surroundings? When I look back at the past few months, I'm able to see so much joy on my part and aside from wanting to get off this stage and hug every single one of you, I will just say that even when I leave events like this and go out with the rest of the world, I don't let them bother me anymore. I'm not perfect by any means but I know now that I've done something that most people will never get to do. I've found a community. I've found a home and I've been able to start becoming who I always wanted to be."

The reaction from the crowd was similar to a rebirth – loud and warm. Feeling satisfied in his honesty, Orion took their enthusiasm at face value. After a quick word from Benny, Orion waved once again and returned to the back room. Altogether, he had been on stage for under ten minutes. The rush stayed with him as he was received in the form of a mass hug from the room's occupants. Orion felt their affection and hoped he radiated the same. He held on tight to an anonymous arm, not just because he felt that he was where he belonged, but because he knew this would be the last show of affection before round two.

Over the next twenty minutes, the back room was alive with the squeak, clip and stretch of different materials. During this time of final touches, some were applying Vivishine to their rubber gear for that extra shine effect, while others were consulting on the best type of conditioner for their leathers.

Orion sat, tinkering with his outfit while participants exited to the stage to a soundtrack of their choice, and then returned. Currently, Pup Chandra was enjoying her turn at centre stage. Orion joined a small group at the door in order to watch. Adding to her existing Regulation K9 ¾ rubber suit, Pup Chandra had added a pair of Mr S leather knee pads, a pair of K9 mitts, and an impressive torquator collar in polished chrome, all paired with her trademark Mr S K9 puppy hood in blue. Always the playful character, she moved and posed to the chorus of Chris de Burgh's *Patricia the Stripper* while volunteers from the audience handled faux dog toys. As soon as the song ended, Pup Chandra sat on her thighs and tilted her head to the audience. Her smile was obvious, even from under her hood. After receiving a scratch behind the ear from Benny, Chandra made further use of the kneed pads and mitts by crawling off stage on all fours before walking upright into the backroom to receive her well-earned kudos.

Next up was Aleksander who, in keeping with his persona, continued to mix the classic Leatherman look with a soldierly flair. Retaining his leather trousers and boots, Aleksander eschewed his more casual leather polo shirt for a military-style leather shirt in red. His well-toned arms sprang like trunks from the short, leather sleeves. Adding to the shirt, he sported a leather vest which he wore open and one well-knotted leather tie in black. In terms of affectation, he had fastened a black leather Sam Browne to run from his right hip, across his torso and to his left shoulder. Finally, perched on his head was a leather, eagle-pin muir cap. The silver eagle in the cap's centre was polished and glistened in the stage lights.

During his time on stage, Aleksander moved like a man in his element, carefully and purposefully. Throughout the entire run of Einsturzende Neubauten's cover of *Sand* by Nancy & Lee, he held the attention of the room with practised ease. Orion, just as transfixed, would later surmise this was an ability gained from years of experience. Slowly, and to the hauntingly hypnotic tones of Blixa Bargeld's voice, Aleksander retrieved gloves from his pocket and placed them on his hands. After that, he knelt and fixed a purposefully undone lace in his boots. Lastly, he walked toward the edge of the stage, removed his hat and handed it to an audience member along with a small cloth he had retrieved from his breast pocket. An initial confusion somehow turned to understanding between the two. The audience member, themselves no more than nineteen, exhaled a life-giving breath onto the silver eagle figure, polished the surface clean, and returned both items to Aleksander who smiled, refastened the cap to his head before standing upright, center stage. With that, the music ended and the spell was broken. Everyone in that room had experienced a shared vision, guided by this modern shaman. Before stepping off stage, Aleksander simply stood silent, his leather shining in the stage lights and his gaze fixed firmly over the applauding audience. Benny knew better than to escort him off. Instead, after two minutes, Aleksander removed his hat, placed it under his left armpit, submitted a small bow to the audience and removed himself. Orion noted that as he walked into the back room, his stride retained the dignity and purposefulness he had displayed on stage. He was, Orion thought, in a different place and in a different time. Aleksander sat himself far from the rest of the crowd and rested while generations of leather culture marinated in his essence.

Just as Orion was standing at the doorway,

surveying the crowd, he was urged to make way. A regal figure, beset with new confidence, was strutting along the length of the back room, through the doorway and onto the stage. Keith showed no hesitation as they planted themselves center stage. What the audience saw, however, was not a figure of expression but one of anticipation. Keith was standing, with no music, dressed in an oversized overcoat. The dark, grey folds stretched from the floor all the way up to cover the bottom of Keith's face. Despite cheers from the crowd, they stood still in the center stage until there existed two seconds of silence. With that, Keith gave the slightest of nods to the DJ from underneath the upturned collar.

The first few guitar chords of *Zombie* by The Cranberries began to emanate from the stage speakers. Keith did not move a muscle. It was only when the other instruments kicked in and the room was filled with a youthful, chaotic energy that Keith reached down and tore the coat from their person like the shameful cover-all it was.

This was not a time for shame.

What stood in front of the crowd was far from the shy, wishful person many of them had met in the past. Keith had made great use of these past eight months. Standing a few inches taller than usual, made possible by the black and neon-green Demonia platform boots, was a figure of brazen exhibitionism. The aforementioned boots were at the bottom of legs dressed only in purposefully ripped fishnet tights. The main item of clothing present was a one-piece leather bustier in black and neon green that reached only so far as to cover politically sensitive areas. Aside, from that, and the pair of shiny, black latex gloves that reached to their forearms, Keith's ensemble displayed more skin than those before it. The reasoning for this was immediately obvious. Keith was adorned with tattoos. Almost every visible inch of their arms, upper body and legs was in close proximity to ink. Some were plain black while some had colour and elaborate designs. Orion's favourite was one just blew the left collar bone which read *Destroy* in instantly recognisable Disney font.

Keith had taken care from the neck upwards as well. Around their neck they sported a black, spiked choker. Each of the spikes stood to a beautifully cumbersome five inches or so. Their face was adorned with a series of piercings not previously seen on their person and their hair, previously worn slick and brushed back, was now wild with black and pink abandon. The look, Orion thought, matched perfectly with the music. In lesser hands, this could have been a plain display of an alternative aesthetic but guided by The Cranberries' music, the kink, punk figure on stage could stomp, thrash, jump and slam along to the enveloping instrumentals and lyrics of violence and loss. This was, Orion also thought, probably his favourite look of the night so far.

Before long, Keith had completed their segment and so, attention finally turned to Orion. He was nervous but not nearly as much as for round one. Indeed, if Orion had to name his current emotional state, he would say that it was one of excitement. He was excited when he changed into his second outfit of the night. He was excited while watching the other contestants on stage and now, he was excited while standing in the doorway, awaiting his cue to step out. The opening of *Wounded* by Third Eye Blind began to play from the stage. Orion was to wait for fifteen seconds before stepping on stage. As he counted to himself, he looked back at his fellow participants, all of whom flashed some gesture of support. Orion smiled at them and stepped out onto the stage.

Unsurprisingly, the crowd cheered as Orion emerged. The floorboards felt firm under his 20-eyelet Doc Marten boots with white lacing. The sturdy but comfortable boots reached up to just below Orion's knees. Finding that too many people had spent time deciding on what manner of pants to wear, Orion was sporting a Mr S leather kilt with accessory pouch. The freedom of mobility it allowed was a refreshing change for him. On his bare chest, Orion wore a Regulation leather H-harness with white piping over which he wore a Mr S Titleholder Bar vest. For affectation, Orion wore a pair of leather police gloves and on each of his upper arms, a white leather bicep strap was wrapped around his sizeable muscle. On his head, he sported a Regulation forage cap while around his neck swung a noticeably thick chain and lock sourced from a local hardware shop.

Orion could not deny that he felt at home on that stage. The cheers from the audience were nourishing to him and with every flex of his muscles, he could feel himself caring less and less that this behaviour was discouraged in the outside world.

Hearing the song coming to an end, Orion was eager to show off one last affectation. Turing his back to the crowd and flexing his arms triumphantly, he revealed the large, white print letters of his own name on the back of his custom-ordered Titleholder Bar vest. The crowd, always hungry for another surprise, erupted into applause. Eventually, but far sooner than he wanted, the song came to an end. Orion waved to the crowd in general and to Goddess Kira in particular, before stepping, once again, into the back room.

There existed a gap of thirty minutes between the second and final round. Orion had used the time to share some kind words with Jamie and Akib, talk amongst his friends and think about the upcoming talent section. Now, with five minutes or so left, Orion sat in the back room, gathering his thoughts. This was, traditionally not always the safest activity for Orion but he found himself rising to his feet as Goddess Kira entered the room.

"Hey, you, how's it going in here?" they asked.

"I'm just loving centre stage. It feels good."

"Ya, I bet it does. I see you out there enjoying yourself. The audience absolutely love you," they said, placing their hands on Orion's hips and drawing him closer.

"I couldn't have done it without you," said Orion, looking into Goddess Kira's eyes.

"Oh, shut up," they responded with a laugh. "Might I remind you that we met in one of the meet-ups. I hardly seduced you into this debauched world. Either way, I want you to know that I'm really proud of you. I think you're doing fantastic and I'm glad that you're enjoying yourself. Now, we're almost at the next round so I should probably get back out front. I just came back here to get this."

With that, Goddess Kira wrapped their long fingers around the large chain around Orion's neck and pulled slowly but with force until their lips met. Orion would have stayed there, with their hand on his chain, for quite some time but as they both had work to do, Goddess Kira released and planted one last smaller kiss before exiting the room.

Orion sat down next to where his gear was stored for the night. In a few moments, he could stand and watch his fellow contestants perform their respective talents. Shortly after that, it would be his turn to stand centre stage, yet again. Orion looked to his left. What was in front of him was the empty section of the room, littered with bags and assorted accessories. What Orion saw, however, was a figure, very much like him, sitting in a bathroom stall, fully clothed with their head in their hands just hoping that no one was taking any note of them. Orion wished so much that he could talk to that figure. He would tell them that everything was going to be okay, that they had the strength to heal and that the future would be better. More than anything, Orion wished he could reach a hand back all those months and pull himself from that bathroom stall into the present, thereby sparing him the pain of uncertainty. This was, however, not the nature of healing. Healing was unknowable and full of hope. Healing was a journey.

Knowing this, Orion looked to his right to a room full of friends and saw a new future figure among them. He was human and imperfect. He was changeable and unknowable. He was submissive and he was strong. He was dominant and he was weak. He was mixed race and he was queer. He, if indeed he still identified as a he, was so many things and would be so many more but the most important thing Orion noted as he stared at this phantom image of the future, was that that he was definitely, fully and joyously alive.

Hearing the noise from the crowd quieten, Orion knew that the last round was beginning. Reaching over to his bag, he retrieved his book of poetry and held its brown leather cover to his heart. Poetry was perhaps not the most expected talent for a contest of this nature, but it didn't matter. His ranking was the furthest thing from his mind. Taking his place at the door among the beautiful, exciting and wonderfully unconventional conventionists, Orion felt at peace and knew that he had already won.

Chapter 11

Wherein we are incapable of caring.

(11)

How had he accumulated so many things? Over the years of living together, Barry had filled his space with gadgets, toys and other distractions. What a waste. What use were they to him now as he absent-mindedly filled two small suitcases in anticipation of his departure from that house? His way through the attic was blocked by several unmarked boxes. Some were filled with obsolete electronics, once considered essential. Others were filled the remnants of hobbies which at one time held his attention. The rest were filled with old clothes which no longer fit. Stacked, cardboard testaments of a body slowly on the decline.

Eventually, Barry reached the instruments of his liberation. Two small suitcases, both small enough to ensure a quick departure, but at the same time large enough for Barry to pack most of his essentials. As he descended onto the first floor of his house (or rather a house that, up to ten minutes ago, Barry had claimed was his), he could hear the complete absence of noise coming from downstairs and knew that Paulina was sitting in the living room gathering her thoughts.

The conversation, if one could attribute such a civilised word to such a dismal interchange, had taken only twenty minutes. Barry had retained the energy built up from his time with Ian. As Barry was the kind of person never to question a barber on an uneven cut, he viewed this retention of nerve as miraculous.

I guess it's easy when it's something that really matters, he had thought. *Also, should I start going to some kind of gay hairdresser now?*

Initially, their conversation had taken a form very much like previous attempts. Forgoing dinner, Barry had confronted his wife in the living room as she slowly Chardonnayed herself through one of her novels. As always, she was warm, loyal and forgiving. Barry knew that he had to get away from her as soon as possible.

After raising the issue, she had responded by reminding him of the needs of the family. Parrying that very predicable first line of attack, Barry insisted that this would be the best move for the family. Next, she insisted upon him the weight and lifelong nature of the wedding vows which he had taken. Barry told her that he had changed (he had not), that he was gay now (just like he was the day he proposed to her) and that he could no longer fulfil those vows. At this point, Paulina, perhaps hardened by repeated escape attempts on Barry's part, was retaining her composure. Barry needed this to change in order for his plan to work. Knowing how sensitive she was about her drinking, he simply waited until she took another sip and then he pounced with a rehearsed, "You become a different person when you drink and it's been happening more and more lately." Successfully turning impenetrable compassion into malleable chaos, Barry ensured that from that point on, the conversation devolved into raised voices and name calling, so much so that he was especially glad that Caroline and Kevin were visiting their grandparents for a few days. After calling him a succession of derogatory names, all of which fell on his ears like a smooth jazz, Paulina had granted Barry the precedent to pack two bags, storm out of the house and call it a day.

The old sociopath switch. A classic.

Walking downstairs with two mostly full carrier bags, Barry knew he still had to retrieve some items from the ground floor of the house. A part of him expected Paulina to be waiting for him at the foot of the stairs. Instead, he found her sitting in the living room with wet cheeks and clenched lips. With minimal effort, he successfully avoided imagining how she felt at that moment. She was silent but Barry knew he was unlikely to make his exit without at least one last round of raised words.

Choosing not to look directly at his wife, he started opening various drawers and retrieving items to add to his escape bags. "I think these few days will be good for both of us. Allow us both to get some space."

Paulina said nothing in response.

"I'm sure that after some thought, we'll both agree on what's best for all of us."

"Yes, and I'm sure that will be exactly what you want and nothing else," she said with the exhausted annoyance of a car crash victim.

Her tone was stunning to Barry. It was new and he didn't appreciate it. She sounded as if she was the one making the risky life change. After all, he was the one leaving his home and venturing out into the world. Still, there would be time to comfort himself later. "I'll come back on Thursday and talk to the kids. We can explain what's happening together."

"You mean that their father is abandoning them?"

"I am not … this … you are making way too much out of this, as usual."

"What would you call it when your father comes home one day, packs his bags and then leaves you and your mother?"

"Look, I'm sure you'll feel—"

"Oh, shut up!" she interrupted. "Just shut up. You always do that, you know. You're always telling what I'll be feeling or thinking or when I'll be agreeing with you. That's how you've lasted this long, isn't it? Whenever you can, you just set your own narrative and work with that. Forget that you lied to me for years, you've been gas-lighting me for as long as I can remember."

"Excuse me, I was not lying to anyone. I wasn't ready to come out and accept who I am. Now I'm doing that and everything is changing for me. You know, I'm not surprised by all this. The guys told me that some people would react this way."

Paulina made a sound that Barry barely recognised as a laugh. "God, you're pathetic. This whole performance is pathetic. The absolute worst thing about this is you actually think that you're the good guy. Some sad, oppressed hero who's coming out into this big world of acceptance like you're some frightened teen when actually you're just an unhappy middle-aged man, and I understand that, Barry, I really do. I haven't been happy in years but I remember the promises I made and I love our children. You? I don't think you know how to love. You'd need an imagination for that."

"Hey, I have imagination. You're the one who wants things to just stay the way they are and we both go forward living a lie. How imaginative is that?"

"We were always living a lie, Barry! At least, I was. I lied to myself day after day pretending that you were a good man and that I could depend on you and look at the coming-out story reward that I'm receiving for my ignorance."

"Story?" he asked. "So, you don't think I'm actually gay?"

"And there it is, you actual, genuine, real-life scum bag. There is the perfect example. You're gay so you get to do what you want. You can be married to me, have children, promise to love me and support me for the rest of your life but because you're coming out, I'm supposed to not just lie down and take it, I'm actually supposed to congratulate your bravery. Of course, you're gay, Barry. I've known for years and long before you told me. That's not the point. It's no more the point than if I had been in an accident or if you suddenly found someone you liked more. The point of all of this, the thing that you have tried desperately not to say, is that you are deciding that your happiness is more important than that of the people you claim to love. Actually, I was wrong before. The absolute worst part of all of this is that it will probably work. Every time you see a Pride flag or hear something supportive, you will actually delude yourself into thinking that it applies to you and that you can count yourself among those people who have actually suffered and fought for their lifestyle. They'll see you and think, what a brave man, coming out so late in life. Do you know what I'll get? Neither do I! Where's my parade, Barry? What do the wives and mothers whose husbands abandoned them do? No parade, no pride and not even any sympathy. If you had just ran off with some young girl, I could at least get some consensus from other people that you were completely in the wrong. Instead, they'll just think about the man following his dream. No one will think about the woman left behind."

Before Barry had even entered the room, Paulina had drawn the curtains. Now, she sat in her regular chair facing the unseen window through which she had gazed countless times as a semi-contently married woman. Aware that she was holding back tears, Barry knew his next words needed to be chosen very carefully. The obvious solution of saying nothing and continuing his packing in silence had completely eluded him. There were several reasons for this, the most foremost of which was that Paulina had been right after all. Barry was unaware of it but something inside him was determined to see Paulina accept his leaving and to view it not as 'abandonment' as she had previously insisted, but as liberation. A healthy person would, perhaps, attempt to minimise the damage they had caused and offer comfort, or at the very least, a swift exit. Barry was not this person, and the fulfilment of this subconscious desire was to be his final, in a relentless streak of victories and matrimony-sponsored indignities committed against his spouse.

He could not leave until she asked him to stay.

"P, I know this is very real and I know we're going to have to figure some stuff out for the kids but I also don't know why you're so upset. You just said you knew that I was gay for years and I stayed with you for all that time. I mean, part of me thinks you're reacting this way because you're a little upset that I pulled the trigger before you did."

Paulina responded to this hypothesis with the silence it deserved.

"Plus, when we first met, you told me how important having children was to you and regardless of how I felt, I promised you that I would make that happen and I did. So, I think I deserve some credit."

Barry could hear the tightening of Paulina's hands as they constricted into restrained fists but aside from that, she didn't make a sound. How could she not say anything? Leaving the house like this would help no one. Couldn't she understand that? Frustrated, Barry resolved himself to continue packing. A silent sparring partner was no use to anyone. "Fine," Barry said, making his way to the kitchen, "but you are not a victim here, Paulina!"

He did not make it four feet into the kitchen before a statement, spoken in a voice filled with resolve, drew him back.

"You abused me!"

Paulina was silent no more and the words fell on Barry like a tumour on an X-ray. In his mind, he was many things but a wife abuser was not one of them. Walking back into the living room, angry and scared, he found Paulina had risen and was standing tall to match him.

"What did you just say?" he asked. "What actually just came out of your mouth?"

"You abused me, Barry, for years. We both know it happened because that's who you are."

"What in the world are you talking about? Have you finally lost your tiny mind? I never hit you once. Take it back!"

"No."

"I said TAKE IT BACK!" he yelled.

"No," she said, standing her ground. "I won't take it back because it's true. You never actually hit me but you abused me. When you treat someone without love or compassion and you minimise their opinion on a daily basis and when you never, not once, go out of your way to make them feel like they're your equal and you make them feel like your unhappiness is their fault and then you put your hands on them and make love to them without tenderness or care or even reciprocation just because it's convenient and they're there, that's abuse. You abused me, Barry, for years. You didn't do it in any way that's illegal but you did it, you sad, bitter, tiny, abusive little man!"

"Oh, I did all that, did I? What about working to buy this house, was that abuse? Or giving you the children that you wanted, was that abuse too? I suppose you're going to say that working my ass off for this family day in, day out for years on end was a form of neglect. Maybe I should turn myself in for providing for my family. I'm sure that would get me a long sentence alone in a jail cell and you know what, I'd rather spend a decade-long stretch making toilet bowl hooch and pretending to a parole board that I found Jesus than spend just one more night in that dull, loveless bed with you. Don't you dare think that you can throw around accusations and paint yourself as a victim here. Do you think staying with me after you knew I was gay makes you a hero? Do you think you're mother of the year award will be here any day now? Well, bad news, everything you did just makes you a coward. A scared, timid homophobe who doesn't want me to be who I am. I'm not scared anymore. This is me moving forward whether your small mind can accept that or not."

Paulina's silence, coupled with the look on her face, led Barry to believe that he had come out on top. If he any sense of the person to whom he was literally married for over a decade, then he knew this was not the case. Paulina's face was not one of admonishment or submission, it was one of disbelief. Shocked, potent and dizzying disbelief at the rampant ignorance and delusion of her own husband.

What could she do? To carry on and try to make him see would be futile. There was, Paulina knew, very little one could do when a selfish person was caught in a momentum of self-righteousness, and Barry was among the most self-righteous people going. Instead, Paulina, long suffering and guilty of nothing but a love for family and a poor taste in men, resigned herself to accepting that Barry would leave her house feeling as though he was in the right. The thought sickened her.

Barry watched his wife, obviously stunned into silence by the conviction of his reasoning, sink into her armchair. He wondered what she was thinking.

An apology perhaps? he pondered.

Paulina could only hold her head in her hand before leaning back in her chair from exhaustion. The sizzle in the room had deflated and both knew that they would never need to raise their voices to each other again.

"Barry, part of you must have known you were gay when we met but you still went full in. You asked me out and we dated and then you proposed to me. I admitted to you that I wanted children and you didn't even question it. You told me you wanted that too and you'd make it happen, so it obviously wasn't a spur of the moment thing. You didn't even give yourself a chance to be single because you had just broken up with someone when we met."

"What's your point?" he asked.

"Why did you decide to marry a woman in the first place?"

Barry moved to sit down but reconsidered as that may be exactly what Paulina wanted. Ask him some questions and get him comfy. Instead, he kept his standing position and answered honestly. "I never wanted to be alone and it was a different time, so it seemed like the best option for carving out some happiness."

"And why did you choose me?"

"I look back and I can't say for sure. I think when I met you, you seemed like exactly what I was looking for in a wife."

Paulina let out a wry laugh. "You know, under different circumstances, that could almost be considered a compliment. Instead, you're basically saying that I seemed like someone you could use up and discard as soon as you got bored and gathered up the nerve."

Barry was beginning to think that she would never see his point of view. Their years together had obviously solidified an image in her head that she was not willing to give up.

Why would someone be so afraid of change? he thought, using the oblivious synapses of his mind.

Whatever the reason for her obstinacy, Barry was growing tired of receiving insults and resolved to recommence his departure.

A cold "I'm going to finish packing" was all he cared to give to her after twelve years.

Within twenty minutes, he was finished. Years of marital bliss washed away by one extended conversation and the convenience of two medium-sized carrier bags. He had not been able to gather all his possessions but he had more than enough for a relatively clean break, if one was content to stretch the definition of the word 'relatively' to extreme lengths. As for more tangible possessions, such as the house and his share of their shared finances, Barry was already planning a call to his solicitor. All that, however, was for a time in the near future. Some great period of scrambling and heated exchanges.

All that mattered now was the exit.

Descending the stairs with his two carrier bags, Barry stood at the front door, removed his coat from a nearby hook and began to put it on. He had performed this action mindlessly and often several times a day for the past several years. Now, as he moved a zip up the length of his torso, he could not but help feel unsatisfied. There existed, in him, a niggling displeasure with how this exit had played out. The feeling gave him a kind of anxious desire that could be felt up and down his spine.

Paulina emerged from the kitchen but did not move any closer.

"Barry?"

"What?"

"Barry, I know you're unhappy. In fact, looking back, I think you've been unhappy since the day I met you. You always seemed to be wanting something better than what you had been given. At first, I thought it was something wrong with me but whether it was food or your job or even me, you just kept on thinking that you deserved more and eventually I accepted that it was just who you were. So, I listened to you complain about friends who had better jobs or people who had more interesting partners. I'll admit that sometimes it worked in our favour and we even managed to carve out a nice little life for ourselves here. I think we all feel that way sometimes but most of us also have an appreciation for the things that we have. We care for the people around us and we don't make light of genuine causes by exploiting them to justify our actions. Still, I know that it's just who you are and you can't help it."

"Are you trying to start another fight?" he asked.

"No, Barry. No. I'm tired of fighting. I ... I just want you to realise that you won't find any happiness out there. You won't be satisfied and you won't feel loved. You're incapable of those things for whatever reason. You'll just keep being unhappy, keep hurting people and keep thinking that there's some better situation you're missing out on. That's why I think you should stay here. We can continue to build the family we started, I can continue to pretend to turn a blind eye and at least you won't have to worry about hurting anyone else. It's the option that causes the least problems for all of us, B."

Satisfaction comes to us in different ways and often for shameful reasons. Barry was not someone who had to worry about shame. In fact, in this moment, he was not worried about anything at all. Instead, he felt a solid wave of vindication. After all, how could all those horrible things she had said about him be true if she was asking him to stay?

Free from the odd feeling running down his spine and fuelled by one last, great shot of delusion, Barry turned silently from his wife, opened the front door, gathered his belongings, and finally made his exit.

He could not even grant her the satisfaction of looking back as he walked away.

"Of course, she wanted you to stay. Not everyone is as adaptable as we are," said Ian, filling two wine glasses with a dark Merlot. "She was probably afraid that she wouldn't get her share of the house or something. I hope she has a good solicitor."

Barry accepted the glass and took a sip. "I'm not going to try and leave her homeless. She's still a great mother even if we're not together anymore. I just think she was afraid of starting her new life but that's okay. I mean, I get how she feels now because it's still fresh but in a few months or even a year, she'll be thanking me for doing the right thing."

"I'm not too sure about that, handsome. Forty-year-old women with two kids aren't exactly the pinnacle of the straight, male fantasy. I think you may have gotten the better end of this deal."

"I always was a crafty dealer."

They were sitting in Ian's apartment. Barry had come to know it relatively well over the past two weeks, in addition to its owner. After leaving the building formerly known as his home, Barry had gone straight there, as had been expected. Without Ian's cajoling, it's possible that Barry would be spending the night in silent solemnity across from Paulina. Instead, he was sipping wine in the mid-size, not-offensively decorated apartment of his first official potential boyfriend.

A marked improvement by anyone's standards and Barry was grateful to Ian for that.

The two men talked late into the night, not just about Barry's recent push for freedom, but also about work, mutual acquaintances and their favourite music. Eventually, after that particular bottle of wine was empty, the two retreated to a more suitable setting. After a period of bedroom embrace, Barry lay in the ruffled sheets of a well-used bed. Ian's arm was around him, holding him close and Barry could not help but think that this was a very good date night and in some ways, the perfect reward for his earlier bravery.

"Barry," Ian began, "you know what you told me Paulina said about you not being happy and not being able to be with anyone? It's not true, right? I mean, I think you're really great and I just don't want this to be the kind of thing where I'm the first guy you're with after coming out."

Even Barry could hear the sincerity in Ian's usually apathetic tone. It was the tone of honesty reserved for lovers in afterglow.

"Hey, that is not what's happening, okay? Ian, I owe you so much. If it wasn't for you, I'd still be sitting in a bar, thinking of ways to build up the nerve to do what I did today. I'm excited to see where this goes because I think you're really great too."

The words were sweet and full of affection and if asked at that moment, Barry could even say that he genuinely meant them. Barry and Ian shared a kiss and reaffirmed their trust in each other, but it didn't matter. The countdown had begun and in the guilt-free machinations of his imagination, Barry was already thinking of something better. A better boyfriend. A better apartment. A better life. Finding it would be easy. Justifying his actions to get there would be even easier.

So, lying in bed, warm and wrapped in the arms of another soon to be victim, *I'm not selfish,* was among Barry's last thoughts before sinking into a peaceful, dream-free sleep.

Free Like You

Chapter 12

Wherein all the
lovers don't
compare.

(12)

Jamie made a mental note to apologise to the taxi driver when they arrived at their destination. In Jamie's supportive but humanely frantic state, they had failed to express their desire to the front of the car with any discernible audibility until the third attempt when 'National University Hospital' was thrown from their mouth with all the impatience one would expect from a soon-to-be parent.

Caoimhe looked at Jamie the way one traditionally looks at a child playing make-believe.

"You know, I'm not in labour, right? I'm not aching or oozing or leaking. Why the rush?"

"I know, I know," said Jamie. "I just want my tone to reflect the situation. Plus, I traditionally take my cab rides in groups of six and usually holding someone's hair back as they lean headfirst out the window."

"What's your point, cutie?"

"My point is that this is my last cab as a non-parent and if I want to be frantic, I will."

Calm as ever, she reached across and grabbed hold of Jamie's hand. "Hey, I'm nervous too but it'll be okay. It's all been arranged."

What could Jamie do but squeeze and smile back.

"You see right through me."

"Like a cheap lace front."

Jamie laughed. "Brilliant. That's the kind of wit I want to teach the little one."

The little one, thought Jamie. *Not so little anymore.*

What had begun with a vibration on the neon-polluted darkness of the reliable nightclub had brought them to this. Reality had followed its instincts, attached itself to the uterine wall of life and split its cells over and over again. Now, the future had taken shape, grown limbs, a small amount of hair and would soon develop tastes, wants, prejudices, dislikes and overly dramatic, taxi-based anxieties of its own.

A kind of manifest biology.

The preceding few months had been deceptively gentle. At several points, Jamie felt that Caoimhe was purposefully sedating their concerns. They loved her for it and the process had undoubtedly yielded positive results, but this kindness was unnecessary.

Jamie was all in.

Gone were the days of our nervous young parent-to-be. What sat in the back seat of that car, holding Caoimhe's hand, was a figure of steel, a reliable procreator and a non-binary person for all seasons.

Even now, as the sights from outside the car whizzed by, Jamie took comfort in reciting the upcoming birthing plan in their head. All other thoughts had been pushed aside for future rumination.

After discussion with her GP and considering the size of the baby along with the current placement of the placenta, Caoimhe had opted for an elective C-section.

Jamie remembered that they had been afraid that Caoimhe would feel ashamed at her inability to endure what someone more callous might refer to as a 'natural birth'. Her refusal to let that manor of self-righteous, old-world thinking affect her mood was one of the many things they loved about her.

Instead, she had taken the initiative and chosen what aspects of the birthing plan were available to her. Caoimhe and Jamie were to meet Caoimhe's parents at the hospital, check in, settle and then prepare for the procedure.

Jamie's parents would arrive shortly after.

Caoimhe herself was thirty-nine weeks along, had the appearance of someone who wished to be de-impregnated and was to appear at the hospital without makeup or nails. Jamie, sympathetic as ever, had offered to arrive in kind, with bare face. Caoimhe appreciated the gesture but gave her permission for just the lightest coat of concealer.

As soon as was possible, Jamie and Caoimhe were to proceed to the operating theatre where anaesthetic could be administered and life, as they both knew it, would be changed forever. As for the procedure itself, Caoimhe had opted for a delayed cord clamping, a gentle C-section and to not observe the birth process. She had originally asked if low, or even dimmed lights could be possible in the theatre. The staff apologised that this was a common request that could not be accommodated.

Lastly, Caoimhe was asked if she wished to choose some birthing music. Looking, Jamie assumed to create an atmosphere of calm and Celtic bewilderment, Caoimhe had chosen some songs by Enya. Jamie had a soft spot for self-made female millionaires and had no objections.

As they approached the hospital, Jamie was grateful that they would have the opportunity to walk calmly through the large, glass front doors to the overworked but reassuringly helpful energy of a front desk, as opposed to bursting through the emergency room entrance like desperate pilgrims. After a quick but sincere apology to the taxi driver, Jamie removed Caoimhe's bag from the rear of the car before opening her door and providing leverage in the form of a sturdy arm.

Both of them instinctively declined to move any closer to the front entrance. Instead, they could only stare at the great glass portal that would lead them inexorably into the future.

"Last chance for both of us to turn around and make a break for it," said Jamie. "After we go in there, it'll pretty much be out of our hands."

"I dare say that I don't think that's quite how it works. We can turn away but we'd still be left with our little milk-hungry friend."

"Speaking of which, I could do with a drink myself."

"How long has it been now?" she asked.

"Over a month. Not a drop. I feel good but a porn star martini could really take the edge off this whole becoming parents thing."

"You think you'll keep it up?" she asked.

"Which, the sobriety or the parental duties?"

"Both, I suppose."

"I suppose it's like all things. I'll keep it up as long as I want to."

Caoimhe gave a playful shove in response to Jamie's terribly unfunny joke as they both built up the nerve to step inside the parent factory.

"I suppose you're right though," said Jamie. "The time for running away has most definitely passed. That time was when you pulled me onto the dance floor all those months ago."

"Ah, I was just trying to get into those incredibly skinny jeans you were wearing," said Caoimhe, getting her own joke in. "You have any regrets?"

"Regrets?"

"About that night and all this and what comes next?"

Jamie looked from Caoimhe's bare but beautiful face to the grey, concrete building before them. "I don't believe in regrets, Caoimhe, and I won't ask you or anyone else if you do because I couldn't care less. I don't regret me coming out to my best friend at ten years old which lead to a bunch of the older boys beating me up and breaking my nose and arm. I don't regret telling people in my life that I love them even if some of them broke my heart. I don't regret trying a stiletto heel for the first time and falling flat on my face on the HIV benefit fashion show runway and I certainly don't regret sharing the dance floor with you to that Kylie Minogue remix."

She was scared. Jamie could feel it. She had a long

day ahead of her and Jamie knew that as well. Nothing to do now but step up and take responsibility.

"So, Caoimhe with the nice nails," said Jamie, presenting their hand to her, "are you ready for one more dance with me?"

Caoimhe smiled and took hold of Jamie's hand as they both walked through the reflective portal and into the hospital reception area.

Caoimhe's parents were waiting on nearby chairs. In the month's following Jamie's second visit to their home, they had all reached a shaky but nonetheless functional symbiosis. Caoimhe's brother, Nathan, was a different story and, true to his word, would not be present for the birth of his only sister's first child.

Joe and Emma rose and rushed to assist Caoimhe who was walking with a sturdy stride. Seeing that she didn't require help, Joe, blessed with a respectable drive to be useful, turned his attention to Jamie.

"Jamie, let me take one of those bags."

Jamie relinquished an over-the-shoulder satchel and the male ritual was complete. "Thanks, Joe. You have any problem getting here?"

"No, none at all. Parking is free in the back and traffic was light. Did you get someone to cover your shift for this?"

"I did, ya, but I had that organised weeks ago. The staff at the salon threw a little party for me a few nights ago and I've been off since then. It was super cute."

Joe inhaled in acknowledgement. A neutral conversation related to traffic and work hours was always welcome when attempting to find mutual ground with Joe. Up to now, it had been the saving grace in repairing their relationship, but Jamie felt that after today's events, they would have at least one additional subject with which to disarm themselves.

"We spoke to the nurse," said Emma. "We're to check in on the third floor and they'll show us where to go and everything."

With that, they were off. A trip up the elevator led them to a friendly administrator at the third-floor front desk. After that, Joe and Emma were shown where they could wait while Jamie and Caoimhe were taken to a separate small room. While there, a nurse outlined the intricacies of the upcoming procedure and where exactly Caoimhe was to stay the night, assuming all went as planned.

After that, a last blood test was to be performed to ensure that Caoimhe was healthy enough to undergo the procedure and the accompanying pain medication. While this was happening, Jamie and Caoimhe joined up with her parents and settled around the bed in which she would spend her night. After a wait of five hours or so, during which Joe was sent for sandwiches for everyone except Caoimhe who was fasting and Jamie, who refused out of solidarity, a nurse returned to the room and escorted Caoimhe and Jamie away. Caoimhe's parents gave hugs to both of them and reassured them that they would be here after.

Before leaving, Jamie could not help but look back at a time when their intention was to shock and confuse this helpful, loving couple. Their aesthetics and values were foreign to Jamie but their love for Caoimhe was not.

Continuing the game of medical musical chairs, Caoimhe and Jamie were taken to yet another room where they were asked to change into medical scrubs for the duration of the procedure. Jamie helped Caoimhe drape herself in the lime green shawl before donning the same garment themselves with the addition of gloves and a medical mask. Catching a glimpse of themselves in the mirror, Jamie could not help but feel some familiar but undeniably unique dysmorphia as if this mirror were transmitting the dimensions, worries and actions of a different person. The Jamie of eight or even five months ago would have wrestled with the urge to slam their fist through the mirror frame and reject the accompanying reflection. The Jamie of the present, however, took a deep breath, swallowed hard and thought of the struggle endured by queer, human rights icon Roger Casement, before continuing with determination.

Walking alongside the hospital bed, Jamie and Caoimhe were led to a small operating theatre. What followed was an hour-long procedure to safely bring life into the world. Caoimhe had chosen to not view the procedure on a monitor, meaning that Jamie was her only source of entertainment. Being aware of this and also determined not to peek below the medical curtain erected to separate members of the public from the medical professionals, Jamie stayed close to Caoimhe's head.

After a while and aided by the ethereal background

of Enya's greatest hits, the entire scene took on an almost tranquil atmosphere. Hospital staff nonchalantly worked their way through a familiar procedure and Caoimhe, anaesthetised but still very lucid, would give the occasional grimace at what she would later describe as "not really pain, more like a tugging sensation".

The only anxiety in the room was emanating from Jamie.

There should be anaesthetic offered to both parents in crazy situations like this, they thought.

Jamie held Caoimhe's hand but could not stop themselves from staring at the pale blue curtain mere feet from their face. There was something afoot behind that curtain. Behind its opaque mystery, Jamie's future was being literally wrenched from the person they loved like some high maintenance rabbit from a magician's hat.

Eventually, the moment of truth came. Somewhere in between one of the songs used in the *Lord of the Rings* soundtrack, the erstwhile tranquil nature of the room was interrupted by new-born cries. Caoimhe smiled and turned to Jamie who responded in kind. After a few more moments, this new, hungry, thirsty, angry, erratic, bitter, demanding, troublesome miracle baby was placed on Caoimhe's chest for skin-to-skin contact while she was stitched up.

Jamie felt a perplexing mix of dizziness, like they might fall to the floor, while also being completely frozen in place.

*****

A filthy bronze coin clinked and clanked its way through the overworked mechanisms of a hospital vending machine until it reached its destination with the manifest destiny of all hospital activity, and a satisfying *clang*. Jamie peered in at the contents that were their meal options. The lettuce on the plastic-wrapped sandwiches was browning with an air of inevitable decay. The high-sugar chocolate options were lined in rows back to front and left to right. They certainly presented a more visually appetising option when compared to their lifeless, BLT neighbours, but Jamie knew that adding sugar to their already worn-out body and mind was asking for trouble. Heeding the advice of their more sensible side, hereby known as their parent mind-set, Jamie settled for an unsalted bag of cashews and sat on a nearby chair to stare blankly at the slightly off-white wall of a hospital corridor.

Just over seventeen hours had passed since new-born screams had first filled that operating theatre. Jamie had accompanied Caoimhe back to her bed for the night where they had close to thirty minutes of privacy before a nurse wheeled their tiny, discoloured, child into the room and placed them in Caoimhe's arms.

What followed was a slow but nonetheless hectic flurry of visitors, both familial and medical, to check up on them, wish them well and offer congratulations. Jamie's body cried out for sleep but could acquire none in the uncomfortable, hospital bedside chair. So, finding no rest, Jamie accepted all guests with grace like some Pharaoh insisting to the world that their lineage shall continue through time.

Now, as they sat in the bolted, plastic piece of furniture, mindlessly shoving any source of protein they could find into their face, Jamie could not help but feel agitated. The dryness behind their eyes was a barrier, holding a series of racing thoughts inside.

"Hey, gorgeous. Ewff, I haven't seen you look like this since the celebratory rave we threw for Coach when she beat her old workplace in that discrimination and unfair dismissal case."

Jamie turned to see Akib walking toward them. "I was happy for Coach and I'd never celebrated someone's legal victory before."

"Well, now you can never say that again. So how are things in there?" asked Akib, gesturing vaguely behind Jamie.

"All good. How did you find me?"

"Find you?" repeated Akib. "I wasn't looking for you. I was on my way to Caoimhe's room. It's just down there, right?

Jamie furrowed their brow in disbelief before turning to look behind them. "What? Oh, God damnit, you're right." In their exhausted state, Jamie had gone in search of sustenance and could have sworn that they had wandered across several floors and down several corridors before finding these precious nuts. Instead, the entrance to Caoimhe's ward was a measly thirty-foot walk away.

"Ready to go back in?" asked Akib. "I'm all charged up to see the little sprog again after heading home for a bit."

"Oh God, in a few minutes, please. My mind is wiped and it's playing tricks on me. Can you come with me for a short walk around the area?"

"I mean, no problem but are you sure?"

"Ya, Caoimhe gave me reprieve for an hour and I just need to clear my head a bit and get some air.".

With that, Jamie walked with Akib down the empty fire escape stairs and into the outside world. The air was bracing and supplied a temporary, cosmetic reprieve from the creeping exhaustion.

Jamie felt different. Jamie was different.

The feeling was difficult to describe but they felt as though they had acquired superpowers inside the hospital and now the previously annoying minutiae of life seemed inconsequential.

"So, sis, shall we wax poetic on the weather or the state of the economy?" asked Akib.

"Actually, how is the economy at the moment?"

"Rushing from one recession to another. Most people are a series of booms and busts, why should our world finances be any different? Seriously though, how are you feeling? We haven't really had a chance to talk alone since the birth."

"I feel happy," answered Jamie.

"Oh?"

"Ya, I feel good. I've felt good since the birth. I mean, I like to think I was prepared for anything but it was a huge relief when everyone survived and I could finally breathe again. No, I feel good but definitely just overwhelmed. The whole thing is so surreal but not scary surreal like Francis Bacon, more fun surreal like early David Lynch."

"Of course, it's weird, you have a baby now. I mean, it's amazing. You're a … are we going with parent or father?"

"I'm happy to stick to parent for the time being and ya, I guess it's pretty amazing," said Jamie, attempting to enjoy the sensual feast presented to them. The light from the sun was gently tingling the sides of their eyes, the breeze was as bracing to their skin as cold water and every shade of colour contrasted against the silver sky and grey pavement. Eventually, the pair turned a corner and sat near a riverbank to watch the ducks flutter across the still murkiness.

"Just to think, less than a year ago, we were in my apartment talking about stuff and now you're actually here."

"I was just scared. I mean, I'm still scared. Absolutely terrified, in fact, but it's a much more manageable type of fear, like I might fail or mess the kid up."

"Or run away in the night."

"Or run away in the night, yes, of course. Abscond away to somewhere warm and be secure that probably no one will guess that I'm running from a woman I impregnated."

"Ya, they're more likely to think that you were the coveted prison wife for some drug cartel leader and now you've ran away with his money."

"That definitely is more in my wheelhouse. Plus, there was all that stuff about being afraid that I was going to miss out and I wouldn't really have a life anymore."

"And all of that is just gone?"

"Are you crazy? God no, I feel it now more than ever, I just don't care as much. I mean, how could I? I get to do something that I never thought I would get or want to do. Overall, I'd say I have around five years of baby bliss before I become bitter and resentful so, here's to being forty-five in my mid-twenties!" Jamie raised an imaginary glass to their own joke. Akib, who was staring at the nothing water in front of them, smiled and shifted as if struggling to speak. "Akib, are you o—"

"Jamie, I want you to know that I'm really proud of you. I mean, both of you obviously, you and Caoimhe, but I really mean it. I don't know how I would have handled all this."

"I think you would have done an amazing job."

"Ya, but that's the thing, I have no idea. I never even thought about it. I know neither of us did so I think I actually wouldn't have been that fine but you, you've crossed this barrier that we didn't even know was there and now you've made new life. It's like you've time travelled into the future and you've made this beautiful thing with a great person in the hope that it will make the world a better place for everyone. I mean, I knew you were shaky and worried at the start but just seeing you now, so summarily into it and ready for whatever comes next, I just think it's really inspirational and I'm super proud of my sister for actually pulling it off."

Tears were already forming in Jamie's eyes when Akib reached over, took hold of both of Jamie's hands and seemed to speak right to their soul.

"Jamie, you are my favourite person and the queer icon I hope to be one day. I love you so much right now."

Jamie could feel the tears running down their cheeks as they leaned in and planted a kiss on Akib who responded in kind. Jamie shifted closer and rested their head against a welcoming shoulder as they felt Akib's arm wrap around them.

They had both endeavoured to live life in the most honest way possible. With independent gumption and with encouragement from each other, they had always accomplished this mission. Through reveals, balls and bashings, they had stood by one another. Now, as they sat on the anonymous and unremarkable bank of a city canal, our two friends held each other close and dared not speak their mutual fear, that they would not see as much of each other anymore. Alongside this fear, however, was the comforting and cemented knowledge that the world was not quite as out of control as they had once thought and that the bond between two people was a beautiful and tangible thing.

In front of them, ducks waddled through the slow, almost imperceptible current of the water and life continued on.

*****

The hallway of the hospital was as busy as ever on Jamie's return but Caoimhe's ward was welcomingly still. Stepping into the privacy awarded by the curtain surrounding the hospital bed, Jamie found Caoimhe deep in a much-needed nap.

Next to her bed was a cot in which lay a wad of blankets and carefree comfort. Jamie peered in to see the angelic figure of their child gently breathing their way through a dream.

They're probably not old enough to tell what's real yet, thought Jamie. *Less than two days old, I bet this whole thing seems like some surreal dream to them.*

Not wanting to awaken anyone from their sleep, Jamie sank quietly into the familiar bedside armchair where they benignly accepted the prospect of another few hours of unsuccessful sleep. This time, perhaps fuelled by the comfort gained from Akib's kind words, Jamie soon found themselves afloat in the smoky and blissful plain of their own subconscious.

After an indeterminate amount of time, Jamie awoke to a new sound. It was the sound of a baby fussing in their cot. As soon as Jamie realised, they were up and at attention. Looking once again into the cot, Jamie could not help but smile as this tiny, fussy human made the smallest of moans and chirps as they stressed their blanket restraints. Looking into their new face, Jamie could make out their own eyes and Caoimhe's chin along with Jamie's mother's mouth and Caoimhe's dad's nose. This tiny human was a tapestry to all who came before it. In their features was contained the genetic memory and experience of generations prior. This child was, Jamie knew, not just their connection to the future but the past as well.

Without hesitation, Jamie reached down and scooped the little bundle into their arms. As they did, Caoimhe, similarly stirred from her sleep and spoke out to them.

"Jamie, are they okay?"

Her voice was slightly weaker than usual. Jamie spoke softly so as to not rouse her further.

"All good on my end. Just going to hold them and rock them for a while."

"Okay, that's good. Hey, it won't be long now and we'll be sent home for some real-life parenting."

"Well, bring it on, I say. I don't mean to sound presumptuous, but I'm pretty sure that we're already the best parents that ever lived."

Caoimhe smiled and laughed just a little, reached out a pale hand and placed it against their face. "Jamie, I can already see that you're going to be really good at this and this is definitely something, at which, it's worth being good."

Jamie leaned in and kissed her. "I love you. Now get some sleep. We'll both be right over there."

As Caoimhe turned and closed her eyes, Jamie sank back into their chair. In their arms was new life and the future incarnate. Jamie could not help but think about what Akib said about making something and sending it into the future. All their life, Jamie had endeavoured to live as genuinely as possible for a world that cried out for change. Now, as they stared into the adorably bewildered face of this new person, they felt resolve like never before.

What audacity, thought Jamie. *What bold-faced diversity and glamour I've weaved into being. This is my child and I love them.*

Gazing with abandon into the hopeful hereafter, Jamie could not wait to bring them to their first Pride parade, teach them the real history of the world or even meet their first romantic interest, if they chose to have one.

With so many moments ahead of them, any negative feelings or inclinations that had occurred over the last few months, seemed to fade away.

Loosening some of the blankets surrounding their child, Jamie soon found a small, newly formed hand reach out and grab onto their index finger. The tiny hand was holding firm a mere few centimetres from Jamie's Coscelia acrylic nails and for a flashing moment, there was no one else in that room. Everyone, including the beloved mother, seemed to disappear and all that remained was the two occupants of that armchair, alone in the cosmos.

Jamie used the time to wipe their quickly moistening eyes. A small, sleepy noise from Caoimhe brought them back to the room. Jamie felt that they could live a thousand years and never be able to repay her for what she had given them.

In their arms, their child was beginning to close their

eyes and for no reason other than they were replaying the memory of that first dance with Caoimhe to the disco-infused remix of a Kylie Minogue classic, Jamie decided to add a quiet lullaby to their steady rocking.

So, leaning back and singing low, Jamie professed to the new and always love of their life that all the hopes and all the pain. All the expectations and all the phantom images of themselves. All the worries and all the lovers. All of that which had come before.

"They don't compare,

To you."

The End

Royce Keaveney

Acknowledgements

I'd like to thank the following people and groups for the following reasons: Eoghan Fallon who is my best friend, Sean Kearns and Pelle Karlsen for helping with the title, Camp Brave Trails for providing a safe and inspirational space for LGBTQ youth, Gabe Cole Novoa who, aside from being a skilled writer, operates a YouTube channel under the name of *bookishpixie* which I would definitely recommend if you want to just listen to someone speak passionately about writing, the Irish kink scene including Handlers and Pups Ireland and the Leathermen of Ireland for inspiring me, and the global queer scene of which I count myself as a proud member.

Royce Keaveney

Printed in Great Britain
by Amazon

23097821R00142